A Christmas Bride

Viveka Portman

16pt

Read How You Want
LARGE PRINT BOOKS, BRAILLE & DAISY

Copyright Page from the Original Book

Title: A Christmas Bride

Copyright © 2018 by Viveka Portman

www.escapepublishing.com.au

TABLE OF CONTENTS

A Christmas Bride
Viveka Portman

Her life is entirely about propriety and conduct, but this Christmas, she will give herself the gift of being wild...

London 1813

Miss Smith is dreading the festive season. With her students gone, long cold days and endless dreary nights are a glum and lonely prospect. So when she comes across a beautiful gown left behind by one of her students, she can't help but try it on. And perhaps a walk down the street as a little Christmas gift to lift her spirits. And a small, warm drink at a local pub. No one will recognise her, and what harm could it do?

Lonely and worried about raising a daughter by himself, handsome widower Robert Carring knows he must find another wife. But having already endured one passionless marriage, he refuses to enter another. He will only marry when he finds the intelligent, spirited woman of his dreams. And then he sees her, making merry on a cold winter night.

Finding herself admired in the eyes of handsome man for the first time, Miss Smith is more determined than ever not to resign herself to a life as a spinster school matron, and makes a daring decision that will change all her Christmases forever.

About the author

VIVEKA PORTMAN is an author of romantic erotic fiction, and has a fascination about times past. With a bachelor degree in anthropology, Viveka weaves historical fact into fiction to create lively, realistic and thrilling tales, sure to titillate and engage the most discerning reader. Considered an upstanding member of society, Viveka does not make a habit of eavesdropping, gossiping or making vulgar displays of impropriety—except, that is, in writing.

If you'd like to know more about Viveka Portman, you can find her at vi vekaportman.blogspot.com, twitter @Vi vekaPortman or like her Facebook page https://www.facebook.com/Viveka-Portm an-1445172812369266.

To all the amazing teachers out there who feel invisible. You're not.

Chapter 1

London, late November, 1813

Miss Ellen Smith gazed around the classroom of Miss Brampton's School for Ladies as a carriage rattled past the window. The glow of the lamps and the hushed murmur of students sewing filled her senses. It was, she must admit, a comfortable place of occupation. The fire kept the room warm, and the well-bred young ladies under her instruction were largely a delight to educate.

Albeit a little dull.

She chided herself for the ungracious thought. A woman of her means was lucky to have such a position. Warm lodgings, good food, a suitable income. She really ought not be so ungrateful.

There was tittering laughter to her left.

Ellen turned and observed the young ladies thoughtfully. Although she personally enjoyed the sound of laughter, Miss Brampton—School Headmistress and Founder, had particularly strict rules about it, and as the girls' educator, she must reinforce them.

Ellen inhaled deeply. 'As amusing as your conversation may be, ladies,' she paused and released her breath, 'you ought sew in silence until it is time to depart,' she reminded them.

The younger Miss Westley's face pinkened, whilst a slight smirk curled the corner of the slightly elder Miss Carring's coral pink lips.

Ellen scarcely withheld a sigh.

Honestly, what did it really matter if the young giggled? They were young women, between twelve and seventeen years; if one couldn't giggle then, when could one?

Still, Miss Brampton's rules *were* the rules.

She turned her attention to the elder of the pair, Miss Penelope Carring. She did look remarkably like her father. Wealthy, widowed and devilishly handsome, Mr Robert Carring visited his only daughter often at the school, and although Ellen would never admit such a thing, she took great enjoyment when he did. She comforted herself in telling herself that her delight was due to the heartening vision of a gentleman so involved with his child. Yet if she admitted the truth, her delight had more to do with the fine square shoulders and thickly muscled calves.

Very muscled calves.

Stop it, Ellen! She chided herself yet again.

Fine calves aside, Mr Carring was good man, and kind father. These were the characteristics that should endear a gentleman to a lady. A woman's feelings really should have naught to do with fine musculature or sparkling handsome eyes.

Yet they did, she told herself with a wayward smile.

Perhaps if she had a father more invested in his family, she would not be mooning over the parent of one of her students. Had her own father, Mr Marshall Smith, not squandered his fortune and left herself and mother destitute, she would never have needed to take employment in the first place. Alas, her father had not been at all like Mr Robert Carring. He had been plump, prone to gout, a drunkard, and a gambler. A terrible collection of humours that had resulted in her current circumstance.

Yet in the darkest, most forbidden part of her heart, her life as a spinster schoolmistress, although comfortable, held none of the thrills, excitement and passion her heart yearned for, especially at Christmas. The long cold nights, and the emptiness of her life seemed only greatened by the festivities of the church and society at large.

Perhaps she was just too fanciful.

Yes, that must be it.

Then why did prayer nor hard work cure her wayward heart of its fanciful desires? Still, she was still luckier than many, however much she yearned for something more.

'Miss Smith?' Miss Penelope Carring called, her slim pale hand raised.

Jolted from her daze, Ellen returned her attention to the child whose dark rampant curls and light hazel eyes were so much like those of her handsome father.

'Yes, Miss Carring?'

The girl smiled, her cheeks dimpling. 'I do believe my father's carriage has just drawn up,' she said and gestured to the window.

Sadly for Ellen, it was the last day of the school term. A day when the students and other staff retreated to celebrate the Christmas season with family and friends.

As a new establishment, funded largely by its headmistress's fortune, Miss Brampton's was unlike many of the educational establishments in London. It closed its doors particularly early, the day before Advent in fact, due to its headmistress's devout Catholicism and general love of the season.

If only Ellen could share that affection. She fairly loathed the empty classrooms and corridors when they left. This year was likely to be even more grim, as it was the first since her mother's passing.

Ellen's gaze turned to the window. Rain splattered the glass, and her heart fluttered. The distinctive black and red of the Carring carriage had indeed just drawn up. She watched the door open, and a tall man duck his head and step from its confines. He smoothed his coat, and glanced to the window.

Cool, dark-fringed eyes met hers through the blur of the wet windowpane. Ellen's throat grew tight and she turned quickly away, fearing the blush that threatened to bloom on her cheeks may be seen.

'I see,' Ellen coughed. 'You may pack away your sewing, Miss Carring, and collect your coat and bonnet, Mr Sneddon will bring your luggage down.'

***

Robert Carring swept inside Miss Brampton's school and dusted a few wet droplets from his hat. They fell like jewels on the highly polished wooden floorboards. He very much liked the school on Hackney Road; its boarding house offered Penelope the home and female company he was unable to provide at their home on St James Street. His wife Mildred had died two years ago and he'd lived a largely quiet life since. He had, thus far, been unable to find a suitable lady who could not only mother his daughter, but also match his passions and interests. He was, perhaps selfishly, utterly unwilling to risk taking on another wife who would bore and disappoint him. Mildred, God rest her soul, had not been the sort to inspire passion, or much else for that matter.

Still, he was a man of honour and had stayed true to his marriage vows, even upon her death. He had not frequented whores as many of his acquaintance did. Their dull, passionless eyes and quickly opening thighs held no charm either—so much the pity.

He wanted a woman of passion, of intellect and spirit.

A collection of characteristics unfortunately absent from society at large, or so it seemed.

Miss Smith opened the door to the classroom and swept into the entry hall, and Robert felt his lips curl into slight smile.

Several strands of golden hair escaped the enormous and frankly unflattering mobcap. The cap was a confounding addition to women's fashion, and if he ever did find another wife, he may forbid her from wearing one. A woman's hair shouldn't be hidden, ever.

Miss Smith returned his smile, and it was impossible for Robert not to notice the way in which her schoolteacher uniform clung to her frame just long enough to offer tantalising suggestions of the rounded charms hidden beneath.

Clearly, he had been alone too long. He brushed his lewd thought away. The ungainly hat aside, he was rather affected by the young schoolmistress. Earnest and clever, she was wasted as a spinster and schoolmarm.

He paused. No, that was untrue. His daughter, Penelope veritably adored her. The school, and Miss Smith's passion for knowledge, was infectious. In fact, if he were the sort of man to be placated by pretty appearance and cleverness, she would, he admitted, make quite a decent bride. However, he was not such a man. He needed passion, he needed thrills, he needed excitement. None of which the clever but damnably straight-laced schoolmistress was likely to offer.

He'd married that sort once before, and found himself badly disappointed. No, if he were ever to take a bride again, it would be for love and passion, not suitability.

'Good afternoon, Mr Carring.' Miss Smith said, her voice soft and breathy.

He inclined his head. 'Good afternoon, Miss Smith, I pray you and Miss Brampton are keeping well?'

Robert had reason to understand that the elderly Miss Brampton was grooming the younger Miss Smith to take over as headmistress of the school. A wise choice to be sure.

She bobbed, 'Indeed, thank you, though Miss Brampton has retired to coast for the season. The winter air in London is terrible for her constitution.'

'It is, I'm sure,' he agreed.

They fell into silence. 'Miss Carring will be with you shortly, sir,' Miss Smith said after a moment, and glanced up the stairwell hopefully.

'Good,' he nodded and appraised her slowly, he had never been able to discern her eye colour beneath the shadow of her cap. He sighed slightly and attempted further conversation.

'How has my daughter fared lately?' he asked.

'Very well,' Miss Smith said quickly, evidently glad to be rid of the awkward silence. She bit the plump lower lobe of her lip. He watched entranced as she released it and continued. 'She excels at Latin, and is the top of her class. Her grasp on the language is remarkable for one of her youth. She would perhaps benefit from paying greater attention during stitch-work, which is, many would say a more useful skill for a lady than Latin.'

Robert struggled to tear his gaze from the wet pink lip as a spear of hot passion shot straight to his groin.

'And do you stitch well, Miss Smith?' he asked, not quite able resist the jibe.

A flash of spirit and mirth dashed across her face. 'Abominably, I'm afraid, but my Latin is exquisite.'

An unexpected chuckle broke through Robert's throat, taking him quite by surprise. 'Then I am once more reassured that my daughter is in sound hands here at Miss Brampton's, for Latin seems a considerably more interesting topic than stitch-work,' he said, wondering if perhaps Miss Smith may be a suitable option for a bride after all.

'Father!' Penelope Carring burst from the room, a veritable hurricane of woollen coats and shawls.

He saw Miss Smith's lips thin, and her demeanour stiffen.

'Miss Carring,' she said with a gentle chide, 'a lady should always deport themselves with care,' she said, and Robert dismissed his earlier positive appraisal.

He noticed, with a mix of disappointment and pride, his daughter slow to a more sedate stride and offered him her hand. He took it and kissed it fondly.

'Penny, you are looking very well indeed. This school must agree with you.'

'Oh yes, Father, it does. I do love it here,' she enthused, her cheeks flushing and eyes sparkling. Robert noticed Miss Smith's lips remain tight, evidently at his daughter's uncontrolled and unladylike enthusiasm. His disappointment grew. He knew that society demanded sedate, controlled women, yet had not a moment ago Miss Smith displayed a modicum of spirit?

Where the devil had it gone?

He threw a sideways glance to check again. Miss Smith's face was entirely shadowed by the stupid mob-cap but her shoulders were taut.

Gone. Just like that she'd slipped into the dull, socially accepted schoolmarm. All evidence of cheer and spirit gone.

It was exceedingly disappointing.

'Miss Smith tells me of your skills in Latin, you must read to me,' he said returning his attention to his daughter.

'Oh, yes, I shall indeed.' Penelope exclaimed and bounced on her heels. 'I should enjoy that very much!' Her ebullient nature was one of the many things he adored so greatly about his daughter, quite the contrast to her dear deceased, but dour, mother. He was pleased that school had not squashed it entirely. As the thought passed, Penelope confirmed his assessment and proceeded to vomit forth Latin phrases loudly and with extreme enthusiasm.

Chapter 2

Ellen was very proud of Miss Carring's skills at language, yet she felt very small indeed as Miss Carring began chattering at volume in Latin, eagerly displaying her budding knowledge to her father. She worried he may be offended by her exuberance. Many gentlemen of her acquaintance found such exhibitionism completely undesirable, particularly in their daughters. In addition, Miss Brampton would see it as an utter failure of her tuition.

No one had ever been able to explain to Ellen why society demanded ladies be quiet and dull, or why they seemed bent on quashing enthusiasm. Yet it was so, and as an educational institution, Miss Brampton's school had to enforce these social mores, and most unfortunately, it was her job.

Ellen stole a nervous glance Mr Carring, whose lips had curled into what she could only presume was a growing snarl of disapproval.

'Miss Carring, please,' Ellen heard herself snap. 'At Miss Brampton's we teach that a lady does not...' Ellen had not finished before Penelope's Latin stopped abruptly, and colour rushed up the child's neck and settled on her already rosy cheeks.

'Oh...' the girl stopped. 'Forgive me, Miss Smith.'

Mr Carring's lips drew thin and a frown drew deep lines between his brows. 'It is quite all right, Miss Smith, I do not mind.' His voice was gruff and irritable. 'I have not spoken with my daughter in weeks. I find her enthusiasm infectious and entirely welcome.' He lifted his hand and rested it on his daughter's slight shoulder. A large carved garnet signature ring glistened in the lights.

His chide made her feel churlish and embarrassed.

'Quite,' Ellen said, though even to her own ears, her voice was tight.

His pale eyes appraised her again, and she wished she knew what thoughts travelled their glassy depths. Then he dismissed her. 'We will depart, and see you in the new year, Miss Smith. Our best wishes of the season to yourself, and Miss Brampton, of course.'

Ellen inclined her head and bobbed graciously, failing entirely to keep the embarrassed bloom from her cheeks.

Late that night, as the last of the students were collected by parents eager to celebrate the beginning of Advent with their families, Ellen closed the door, listening to the last carriage rumble down the street.

'Have you eaten, Miss Smith?' An elderly dry voice came from behind. Ellen startled, sending the oil lamp swinging and turned to see old Mr Sneddon, the housekeeper's husband and the school's butler shuffle in.

'Yes, I managed something between Miss Westley's parents' arrival and Miss Grainger's.' She said, 'I will retire now, you may lock up,' she said and lifted her skirt to make her way up the stairs to her room. 'Good night, Mr Sneddon.'

Mr Sneddon coughed, drawing her attention back. 'I had Milly sweep the dormitories, and she noticed someone's left clothing in the wardrobes,' he said as she made her way up. Ellen felt her face crumble into a frown.

Another teaching failure.

'How such girls will ever manage their own households, I will never know,' she sighed, 'Very well, once I am certain to whom they belong, I will have them returned in the morning,' she said.

'Very good,' Sneddon said. He paused and coughed again. 'This your first Christmas since your mother's passin', isn't it?'

Ellen's heart squeezed and her eyes pricked instantly.

'Yes,' she said and looked over the banister at him, offering what she hoped was a brave smile. 'It is.'

'You'll be coming to mass with Mrs Sneddon and I then over the season?'

The thought of sitting in the freezing church, listening to long droning sermons with only Mr and Mrs Sneddon for company was a horrifying reality she knew she'd have to face.

'That would be lovely,' she said stoically. 'Thank you.'

Mr Sneddon's face crumpled into a smile wreathed in wrinkles. 'Excellent, we couldn't have you attending alone, of course.'

'No, I suppose not,' Ellen replied, when honestly she hadn't planned on attending at all. 'You really are too kind.'

'Well, Miss Smith, goodnight,' he said and shuffled to the front door and latched it securely as Ellen fled upstairs.

When she reached the first landing, she was near tears.

Spending Christmas with the Sneddons! What a terrible thing! Even though her mother had been impoverished by her father's death, at least she'd been exemplary company. Her mother had been a lively, bright spark, until consumption had leached the spirit and life from her. Her mother had been so unlike the Sneddons, who although meant well, were as dry and dusty as the rugs they beat, and the mantels they polished.

Ellen bit her lip, cursing her uncharitable assessment of the elderly couple who had shown her nothing but kindness. She sniffed and walked into the dark dormitory to ascertain to whom the left clothing belonged.

It was cold up there, the fireplace burnt out and empty. If she hadn't known better, she could have thought the room had been abandoned months, not mere hours before. The thought depressed her.

The oil lamp sent a warm halo of light around the room, making shadows dance and disappear as she moved forward towards the row of wardrobes to assess the forgotten clothing.

Her fingers grasped the icy brass knob of the first wardrobe, and she pulled the door open. It gave a loud protesting squeak, but was empty.

The second revealed more of the same. Finally, she came to the third wardrobe and pulled it open. Inside there was a beautiful gown, one that most likely should have been taken home with great care, rather than folded in luggage. Perhaps that was why it had been left to hang, and then overlooked in the rush to depart.

Even in the dim light Ellen could see that the gown was deep brown, striped with gorgeous gold thread. It was Miss Pickering's gown, she recalled; the young lady had worn it out on an evening excursion to the orchestra a few months before. She had admired it then, and admired it more now. The young lady would certainly be missing this dress if she didn't send it home on the morrow. Ellen's fingers lingered over the long gold threads. Miss Pickering was about her height, and well developed for girl of ten and five.

Ellen bit her lip guiltily as she assessed it for size. She knew the gown would fit her just as well as the young Miss Pickering, or perhaps even better.

It was a terrible shame she could never afford a gown so fine. Indeed, her best gown was positively dowdy by comparison, yet had cost her months and months of wages to save for.

And even if I had a gown such as this, where would I wear it?

Nowhere, that was where.

She had no chaperone and no great means to be invited to the occasions that might warrant such a dress.

Yet she couldn't force her fingers to quite let go of the fine material, or ease the mounting beat of her heart at the notion of trying it on.

The thought was fanciful, ridiculous. What if she were discovered doing such a thing? The humiliation would be devastating.

Although ... it was unlikely that she would be discovered. Mr Sneddon and Mrs Sneddon had a cottage at the rear of the schoolyard, and were unlikely to return to the schoolhouse once Mr Sneddon had locked up.

Her heart beat a little faster. The wicked opportunity to try it on was so tantalisingly close it was maddening.

What harm would it do?

She could simply try it on, then take it off again.

After all, she may never have another opportunity to try on a gown such as this. Tomorrow she'd have to ask Mr Sneddon to send it back to Miss Pickering.

She bit her lip and her breath quickened with excitement.

No one would ever be the wiser, and what harm would it do?

Quickly she closed the door to the dormitory, and placed the lamp on the bedside table, then hurried back to the wardrobe. Without allowing her conscience to put in another complaint, Ellen pulled the dress from the wardrobe and draped it over the bed nearby. It looked even finer out of the wardrobe, the gold glittered brighter in the lamplight and her skin prickled in anticipation of feeling the smooth cloth slip over it.

With fingers that trembled slightly, she unclasped the front clasps of her own gown. She'd long dispensed with gowns that required a maid to lace or button at the rear. There was no room in the life of a schoolmistress for maids.

She had noticed buttons on the front of the beautiful gown immediately; small, pearl and gold, they were a stunning feature to the bodice.

Her own prudishly high-necked schoolmistress's gown slipped from her shoulders and she pulled it from her arms. The cold dormitory air licked around her body as the rest of the gown fell to the floor and she stepped from it. Now, dressed only in her chemise, the cold truly began to sink into her bones, soaking through the thin muslin despite the snug fit of her quilted stays. Gooseflesh erupted over her suddenly exposed arms and Ellen moved swiftly to lift the beautiful gown over her head and slip it on. It was not as easy as she had hoped. Despite its front-facing buttons, this gown was indeed made for someone with a maid to assist in dressing. Still, after a momentary struggle, Ellen pulled her way through the layers of gown and slipped her arms through, finally emerging and pulling the gown down straight. The scent of the Miss Pickering's perfume still lingered on the fabric as Ellen deftly re-buttoned the gown. As she looked down she admired, just briefly, the full swell of her blue-veined breasts as they rose and fell over the gold fringing of the bodice. Her body clenched unexpectedly at the sight of them. She had always known her figure was a fairly fine one, and secretly lamented the fact it would never be explored by a husband.

Really! She cursed herself, *you do think the most vulgar things.*

Slowly, Ellen lifted her head and looked across the room at her reflection in the mirror. The mob-cap, an enormous white thing that Miss Brampton insisted all female staff wore, clashed with the deep brown and golds of the gown. With more than a little pleasure, Ellen pulled it from her head, allowing her hair to cascade free in a riot of golden curls.

For a long few moments, Ellen stared at her reflection, finding herself almost unrecognisable, even to herself. Her body was embraced by the magnificent gown, its palette of colours complementing her creamy complexion, whilst her hair, always hidden by the muslin and lace of her cap, shone free in the flickering lamplight.

It was vanity, to be sure, to admire herself so. Still, God may strike her down there, and at least she'd make a pretty corpse.

Ellen did a little twirl in front of the looking glass to see just how fine she appeared.

The figure in the mirror moved with grace and a style she hadn't quite known she'd possessed. What a pity it was to be locked in here, unable to shine, even if just for one night.

Circumstance had made sure that Ellen had always been neatly, if not well dressed. Her mother could not afford fine gowns; instead Ellen had always been supplied with sturdy clothes that would last and keep her warm. Her uniform at Miss Brampton's was no different. Well-made and comfortable, her school dress was the image of practicality. Quite the opposite of this one. The magnificent autumnal gown was made to draw the eye and make the wearer feel like a princess. Designed for the cooler autumn weather, the sleeves were long, and the rich fabric heavy. Ellen sighed, wishing she could, just once, wear such a fancy gown out and perhaps capture the eye of a smart gentleman, who would fall desperately in love with her, marry her, and whisk her away to live in his large estate in the country.

Such dreams were silly. She was an impoverished schoolteacher, hardly a desirable catch.

Still. A lady could dream.

What would it feel like to be seen in such a fine dress?

What excitement would rush through her veins when she caught the admiring flash of a gentleman's eye?

She laughed softly to herself and swayed once more in the mirror.

It would be a very nice Christmas gift indeed, to be looked at with admiration rather than pity.

Slowly Ellen's gaze drifted to the window and its thickly drawn curtains.

She could just take a very quick turn about the street, couldn't she?

What harm would it do?

It was not so late that it would be dangerous, not near the school at least. She could hear carriages rattling by and the chatter of people going about their business before the lamps were extinguished. She knew for certain that the teashop next to the pub would still be open, catering to those returning from the opera or theatre.

She bit her lip; was it silly to want to go out, dressed finely and pretend, for just one moment, she was someone other than Miss Smith, schoolmistress at Miss Brampton's?

She knew the answer, yet it didn't stop her from grabbing her reticule and a few coins from her room and slipping back down the stairs to unlock the front door.

Chapter 3

Mrs Mathers, the housekeeper, had taken Penny upstairs to bed, and Robert reclined in the sitting room of his luxurious St James Street terraced home. He sipped his whisky thoughtfully, then placed it down, rose and walked to the fire. He stood before it and stretched his hands out, feeling the warmth lick at his palms as the orange and gold flames danced and jumped.

He was bored.

So bored.

Penny's return had been a delight, but she'd fallen asleep halfway through supper, and it wasn't right to keep the poor child awake simply for his own entertainment.

The mantel clock tick-tocked with tedious monotony.

It was not yet late, and it was too early to retire for the evening.

Robert supposed he could take the hack to Mr Thomas Porter's home and have a game of cards. Thomas was wild for cards. Yet the thought of listening the gentleman's long vulgar litany of recent sensual conquests didn't inspire him.

Especially since he had not had any conquests, sensual or other, since Mildred had died.

Guilt swooped in his belly. Mildred.

How often he thought ill of his departed wife.

Truthfully, she'd been a good wife. Good in that she'd lay with him when he wished, bore him a healthy child and had kept a good home. She did not deserve his scorn, yet her death had left him desperately yearning for something more than the stale, dull drudgery that he had known to be marriage.

He knew he needed to marry again, to mother Penelope, to beget an heir for his household, and to ease his own sensual frustration, but he could not, *would not,* lock himself into a purgatory of boredom again.

He walked to the window and stared out at the streets. There were a number of gentlemen's clubs on the street, and most were opening for their night of business. He felt the familiar frustrated burn of lust stir in his breeches. It would be so very easy to go there and slake his need on a willing courtesan or whore.

He shook his head and reached over for his whisky and sipped it again.

No, he was a man of morals and integrity. He would not pay for sensual favours. Perhaps a walk would clear his head.

Yes. That would do nicely.

Without any further deliberation, Robert rang the bell. Mr Potts, the butler, arrived moments later.

'I am going for walk,' he declared. 'I need to stretch my legs and get some fresh air.' The butler looked sceptical, but nodded.

'Shall I get your coat and hat, sir?'

'Thank you,' Robert said.

A few moments later, Robert found himself briskly walking the streets of London. It was busy, there were street sellers still abounding and music poured from the doors of public houses and gentlemen's clubs, making him feel more alive than he had in years.

Over an hour passed as Robert meandered through London, taking in the sights and sounds, finding himself drawn deeper in the city. He was about to turn around when he recognised Miss Brampton's School for Ladies. Lost deep in maudlin musing, he'd walked nearly four miles. He rubbed his chin and glanced up at the dark windows of the school. All the students would have returned home, and the staff would be abed no doubt. He mused, his mind drifting to the sweet-faced Miss Smith, before dismissing it curtly.

Clever but passionless, he reminded himself.

It was foolish for him to have walked this far, the evening was getting late and no doubt the lamps would be out soon. He glanced about, considering hailing a hack. Many people still strolled the streets, and the night, though cloudy, was still clear. He inhaled, smelling pipe smoke on the cold air, and decided to walk home instead.

Robert slowly walked down the street. He walked past a teashop; a few patrons still sat in the warm glow of the store, sipping tea and eating cake. The sight made him realise he was quite parched from his exertions. Beside the teashop was a public house, cheerful fiddling music beckoning him in from the cold. A nice ale would set him up nicely for the long walk home, he reasoned, and the brew would likely help him sleep when he finally did retire for the evening.

Robert stepped up into the pub, and he was met by ribald laughter and much chatter. He gazed around the room; it was very dimly lit indeed. Only a few oil lamps lit the bar, but in the corner he could see the musicians playing for a rapt audience and a small group of dancers.

Robert walked to the bar and greeted the bartender. The barman was grizzled, with wild bushy eyebrows that collapsed at Robert's appearance.

'Your finest ale,' Robert said over the music.

The barman nodded and poured a tankard of rich amber fluid.

'Your musicians are doing a fine job,' Robert commented and handed over a few coin.

'Aye,' the barman agreed, 'it's not every night we get 'em in, but tonight we've even got people dancin',' he said. 'Good to see them young folk dancin'.'

Robert wasn't entirely sure how one would dance to the fast-paced fiddling, but he took his tankard and began to walk towards the dim corner where musicians and dancers were surrounded by crowded tables. It was then he saw a vision.

Golden hair flashed in the lamplight as a young woman spun wildly in time to the music, causing hoots and cheers from the onlookers. Robert smiled at the sight and sank down on the nearest stool and watched. The woman was clad in a fine gown, clearly a lady of some means. Her dress hugged the curves of a perfectly formed body. Robert sipped his drink, but found his throat thick when the young woman lifted the hems of her dress and began a complicated series of folk steps in time to the music.

Robert felt his groin swell at the sight of fine and narrow ankles. It was a rare pleasure to see a woman enjoy herself so honestly. He looked about to see who was chaperoning the woman, but any number of the women or gentlemen watching could hold the position.

He watched entranced as she danced on, swaying, tapping and moving to the fast-paced rhythm with absolute abandon.

Finally, the reel ended and the young woman took a sweet curtsey. Robert found himself cheering her efforts and clapping with other patrons.

The woman took a second curtsey and moved towards a table. Robert glanced at the other onlookers, noting he wasn't the only one watching her so intently. Several of the other gentlemen's eyes followed her with avid attention.

She began to move through the crowd. Her features were shadowed by the poor lighting but Robert was under no illusion she was very pretty indeed.

A young man, dressed in worn but well-kept attire, rushed forth and took her hand and led her to a table. The young lady sank down and mopped her forehead with the back of her hand as she accepted an offer of a tankard of ale.

A surge of concern, and perhaps a little jealousy, swelled in Robert's chest. His waistcoat grew tight. What kind of chaperone would condone a lady drinking ale? Certainly none of his acquaintance. He looked around the congregation, trying to decipher to whom the young lady belonged. No one appeared overly concerned for her welfare and the irritating sense of concern swelled again. Perhaps this was quite the usual circumstance on Hackney Road? He was, after all, far from his side of London.

***

Ellen's head was spinning, she knew she ought not partake in any more ale. Yet what a treat this was! The music, the gentleman and the dancing, she'd never thought life could be so much fun. The young man offered her his hand, but she shook her head and patted her forehead again to dab at the perspiration that glowed there.

'Where are you from, miss?' The young man asked. 'I ain't seen you abouts afore.'

Ellen was about to answer something particularly witty when she looked up and caught a handsome pair of eyes at a distant table.

The man, heavily disguised by the dim lamps, was watching her with a hungry, hooded stare.

Her body thrummed. This night was a night of firsts. Until now, she had never received such appreciative and suggestive glances and though her mind didn't quite know how to comprehend them, her body seemed to respond in the most primal and thrilling way.

She bit her lip, unable to tear her gaze from the gentleman at the distant table. There was something familiar about the hooded eyes and the angle of jaw, but she couldn't quite place it. Lost in thought, Ellen couldn't hear the continued conversation of the young man and her ale remained untouched. Under the gentleman's continued gaze, moisture filled her mouth and down below her waist; her secret most feminine flesh seemed to heat and melt.

Goodness!

Even when she lifted her eyes boldly to meet him, the gentleman did not defer his gaze. Instead, he lifted his own tankard and raised it to her. The liquid glinted as he tilted it, sloshing a little over his long fingers. A dark signature ring glistened in the lamplight.

The man's lips curled into a smile and, he brought the tankard to his lips and gulped long and hard.

Her stomach leapt into her throat. The man *was* familiar—it was Mr Carring!

Heat and fear rushed through Ellen's body all at once.

What was he doing here? Did he not live far away?

She couldn't break the stare, even though if he discovered her identity she may lose her position and honour.

She ought to leave immediately, yet remained frozen to the spot.

'Miss? Ye or'right?' the young man beside her asked, his hand once more hovering dangerously close to her own.

Ellen slipped it away, felt herself nod in lieu of answering. She fumbled for the previously neglected tankard of ale. She brought the liquid to her lips and gulped it. The ale was sweet and bitter, and she nearly gagged. The mouthful did nothing to ease the tightness in her belly.

The young man frowned, he spoke again.

However, to Ellen, time seemed to slow. The musicians began to play another song, this time slower and somehow more intimate. She glanced up and found Carring staring at her again.

I must go! Ellen thought frantically. She made to move and slightly knocked the young gentleman in her haste, her skirts twisted around her legs. At that same moment, she saw Mr Carring rise, his eyes never once leaving her.

He began to approach. His gaze burning. He looked lithe and powerful, like a lion stalking a startled deer.

Her heart was beating powerfully now, its rhythm matching the rapid madness of the fiddlers.

She turned, moving away from Carring.

It was imperative she escape and return to the school at once. She had to disappear into the crowd, slip away. Muttering an apology to her confused young suitor, she pressed into the crowed, hoping to disappear into forest of bodies, when she heard a gentle cough beside her.

'Are you free to dance?' Mr Carring's smooth voice sent gooseflesh rippling up her back.

Ellen turned, terrified he would discover her identity, then looked up.

His face was as handsome as ever, but the hungry expression was etched deeply into the lines of his face as if with an artist's chisel.

There was no recognition in his gaze, nothing but frank, honest admiration.

The flesh between her legs tightened and her breasts heaved.

For just a moment her tongue remained captive by her sudden and unbidden desire.

She should say no. This was a foolhardy game and one she could only lose.

And yet her recalcitrant tongue would not form the refusal her common sense bade.

Carring had not recognised her. *There was no danger.* He would no more expect to see Miss Brampton's schoolteacher in this public house than he would expect to see the Prince Regent.

She bit her lip and felt herself nod.

She could feel his gaze on her lip, and thought she heard the slightest moan of need.

He needed no other confirmation.

Ellen felt his hand press into her forearm, hotter than any brand. Smoothly he drew her to him and pulled her into the circle of dancers.

Ellen shivered despite the heat. The mere touch of his hand on her cloth-covered arm made her body nearly crumble and she feared she may fall apart all together.

The fiddlers exploded into yet another song and Ellen could feel the music inside her. Her flesh thrummed with the beat, and her mind emptied of doubts.

Under Mr Carring's firm guidance, her feet followed his steps into a folk dance as if they'd been born to it. They swayed and stepped in perfect unison. She could smell the scent of him at this proximity. He smelled smoky, masculine and charming. Perhaps it was the ale, and her body so unaccustomed to the closeness of a man, but she felt wonderfully, irresponsibly wild and free.

The small irritating complaints of her common sense fell silent under the weight of his hand on her waist and the encouraging cheer of the music.

And still, she wanted more.

Just for this one night. She would take more.

This would be the most thrilling Christmas gift of all.

Ellen swayed with him as his hand tightened on her waist. She could feel each finger press into her soft flesh.

Her breath caught and she stumbled slightly, leaning closer to him and pressing her breasts against his chest.

Was it terribly wicked that she wanted his hands on her more than for just this modest dance?

Too soon, the song ended and Carring stepped away slightly and bowed regally. 'Forgive me, I have not enquired as to your name, and we have had no formal introduction.'

Heat licked the length of her neck as he waited for her response.

His eyes were hooded, still hungry, admiring and desirous.

Her nipples hardened beneath her quilted stays.

It took her a few moments to find an answer.

'Tonight I have no name,' she whispered, unable to completely find her voice. 'This night is a Christmas gift to myself, to do as I will.'

She looked up to gauge his reaction. He stiffened. The Adam's apple in his throat bobbed as he swallowed.

'How unusual,' he murmured, and he stepped in closer. This time Ellen felt his fingers move on her back, drawing her indecently close. Now she could feel the thickness rising in his breeches. A thickness she'd only ever heard whispers about, but never actually encountered.

He gazed down at her, 'Then tonight may just be a Christmas gift to myself as well.'

He pulled her into another dance and Ellen and Carring found themselves once more consumed by the music and a mutual desire for freedom. If someone had asked Ellen how much time had passed, she could not have answered, until the barman tapped them on the shoulder and suggested they end the evening and depart.

'I had no notion it was so late,' Ellen breathed. The colour roared into her cheeks. 'I've never had such an evening in my life, I've never felt so very ... free.' She sighed, 'Thank you for your company.'

Carring had said nothing for a long time, but his dark-fringed eyes seemed conflicted.

'I ought to leave,' she said, knowing she need not leave. The Sneddons would not miss her until breakfast. Thus it was entirely possible for her to spend the entire night dancing, if not here, elsewhere.

'Allow me to escort you home?' Mr Carring asked, taking her elbow gently and turning her towards the door.

Ellen felt her body clench again at his touch. It was ridiculous to feel such things for a man she scarce knew and had who had no idea who she was, yet it was thrilling.

The wind had risen during her time in the public house, and a few raindrops began to fall. She had brought no shawl and the icy droplets stung the swell of her breasts. She inhaled deeply and hesitated.

'I need no escort, thank you,' she said softly, 'My home is not far and I should like to relish my freedom just a few moments longer.'

'Have you enjoyed yourself then, this evening?' Carring asked, his grip tightening slightly on her elbow. She hesitated, not willing to leave just yet.

She looked up into those gorgeous pale hazel eyes, so deeply shadowed by dark lashes. 'More than I could ever have hoped,' she breathed.

Chapter 4

Robert didn't know what he was doing; the sweet, fresh scent of her hair, and the warmth of her skin beneath the fabric of her dress was driving him to distraction. All evening long he'd been grateful for the full coat he wore to cover the raging height of his erection.

He must be mad.

Educated and softly spoken and dressed so finely, someone would be looking for this young lady, certainly.

Someone, somewhere, would miss her.

He chastised himself for his brash and forward manner with her. He ought to be appalled by her wilful disregard for societal norms and rules, but her fierce determination to experience an evening free from a chaperone amused and excited rather than horrified him.

If he were any type of gentleman, he should be demanding her address, marching her home and returning her to the bosom of her family.

Bosom, he looked down at the swell of her breasts, the raindrops looked like diamonds against the creamy fullness. She looked up at him, opening her mouth to say something more. Her lips were pink and moist. So touchable, so very kissable.

I should not.

But he did. He kissed her, hard.

His mouth met hers in a sensual crush, and he felt her gasp. His hand left her elbow and curled around her waist, drawing her to him. She mewed softly in her throat.

What the devil was he doing?

Her small frame melded to his like soft molten gold, and Robert felt a low growl of need grow in his throat.

He should take her home...

His hands travelled from her waist and cupped the round, firm globes of her buttocks.

She gasped, and he expected her to push him away, chastise him, *anything.*

She did not. Instead, the woman pushed her body into his and he could not help but grind his cock against the warm softness of her belly.

His hands kneaded her buttocks and she whimpered, not in pain, or fear, but pure need. The sound was a spear of pleasure straight to his groin.

'We must stop,' Robert heard himself gasp, his voice gruff with pleasure.

'No,' she whispered, 'Oh no, don't you dare.' Her lips moved along his cheek.

His cock strained harder at her demand.

'This may be my only chance, to ever...' She whispered, but he did not need her to finish. He kissed her into silence, guiding them both into the dark privacy of the alleyway between the public house and teashop.

***

Excitement pulsed through Ellen's body in hot waves. It was dreamlike. She felt the cold bricks of the teashop behind her back as Carring pushed her against the wall.

'Is this what you want?' his voice was ragged and he kissed the skin of her neck, sending ripples of pleasure down her body. 'Truly?'

'Yes,' she murmured and kissed him again. There was nothing she wanted more than for this pleasure, this excitement to continue.

'Then I will give you a Christmas gift you will never, ever forget,' he growled.

He moved from her. Ellen felt loss of heat immediately as his body pulled away. The chilly air wrapped around her body, as the cold damp bricks sapped the warmth from her back. She looked down, and found Carring knelt on the damp cobbles before her, his hands at the hem of her skirts.

Confused, her hands flew to his shoulders, 'What are you doing?' she asked as she felt his hands slip beneath the fabric and skim the length of her calves. 'Do you not need—' she didn't finish, her voice disappeared into a surprised gasp as he lifted her skirts and his hands seared a path above her knees. His hot fingers danced along the sensitive flesh of her thighs, parting them. Then she felt his lips, gently kissing the path so recently forged by his fingers. She swallowed and felt her pulse hammer in her most private of places as his kisses and touches drew closer. His hand flittered past the curls of her sex, seeking, and gently caressing. She moaned, the sensation exquisite.

'Oh,' she murmured unsure of herself. Her body was wanting more, but more of what, she could not quite place. She knew of what men and women did in the marital bed, but this was no marital bed, and they were certainly no man and wife.

His fingers urged her legs further apart, and as they did, she felt him part the curls of her womanhood, seeking the moist flesh of her sex. She shook, the sensation so delicately sweet, but intense. He kissed her thigh and then she felt something hot lick the length of womanhood. She cried out and her hands involuntarily moved to Carring's shoulders and curled themselves in the hair above his collar. His tongue flicked again, from her secret opening to the hardened bead at the top.

She hadn't known such pleasure could exist. On his next stroke he thrust his tongue into her, and she knew she was only just discovering the pleasures that could be had. She shuddered as the coarse skin of his cheeks grazed the flesh of her thighs as he thrust into her over and over with his tongue. Her fingers coiled in his hair and she widened her legs to allow him deeper access. As he continued to lick and thrust, Ellen found a warm weight growing in her womb. It was incredible, *he* was incredible. All the silly innocent fantasies she'd had over the years paled to insignificance as Mr Carring licked, thrust and then sucked at the folds of her womanhood. His hands gripped her spread thighs and a spear of sweet ecstasy shot through her entire body, then broke like a wave over her. She keened and gripped his hair tightly as her body met with passionate crisis. Ellen's legs trembled, and it was all she could do to stop herself falling to the ground.

After a moment, she felt rather than saw Mr Carring move to stand, and her skirts tumbled to cover her spreadeagled legs. She clenched her eyes closed, revelling in the aftershocks of pleasure, and heard the ragged sound of his breathing and the pop of buttons opening his breeches.

Ellen couldn't believe he'd given her such pleasure, and as her body shook with one more spasm of pleasure, she realised he must have his too.

She kept her eyes tightly closed, and heard the sound of fabric being pulled down his legs.

'Open your eyes,' he murmured, 'Your beautiful eyes.'

She did. Mr Robert Carring stood before her, his handsome face hungry and dark with need. Ellen swallowed as her gaze travelled south, and saw through the darkness of the alley his manhood standing firm and erect.

Her mouth dried; his implement was large though she had nothing to compare it to. It was foreign, strange but thrilling in its primal beauty. She reached forth and ran a tentative finger over its swollen head. It came back moist. She bit her lip, it was impossible that such a thing would fit within her.

'What am I doing?' she gasped.

Mr Carring smiled, his teeth flashed in the dark. 'Whatever you wish...' he murmured, and brought his mouth to her neck, and kissed.

How is it possible to feel this kiss on my neck as well as between my legs? she mused as she threw her head back, exposing her neck to his wandering lips. Her sex pulsed anew.

'Do you want me?' he growled softly, and nipped the delicate skin beneath her ear.

She remembered the magnificence of his cock, 'Oh yes,' she moaned.

It was all the consent he needed. Carring's hands reached for her skirts again and pushed them high. The cold damp air whipped around her.

With his knee, he parted her legs again and this time the cold air licked the wet lips of her womanhood.

Ellen opened her eyes as his mouth left her neck. Her gaze followed his and she watched his free hand grip his cock and guide its thick head to the opening between her legs.

She must have whimpered, for he paused, shushed her with a gentle kiss.

She looked up at his face, his brow furrowed in concentration. She could feel the hot burn of his manhood's broad head push gently upward.

Ellen shuddered, she'd heard about the discomfort first sensual relations could cause a virgin, but she was ready. She may never have the opportunity again.

For a time, he rhythmically pushed gently and insistently upward. The blunt thick head nudging her, coaxing her to open, but he did not yet breach her maidenhead.

She sighed, relaxing slowly into the strange urging.

Was this what sensual relations were?

Was this all?

He growled softly under his breath.

'You have never been with a man before, have you?' he whispered.

She hesitated, not entirely willing to disclose, then he nudged a little harder.

A sharp pain shot through her core. 'Oh! No,' she whispered, 'I have not.'

The nudging between her legs stilled for a moment.

'You still want me?' His voice cracked under the intensity of his words.

'Yes,' she said quickly. 'Yes.'

He pushed a little harder, and she winced just slightly.

'You may feel discomfort,' he warned, pulling back just a fraction.

'I know,' she said.

He pushed with even more pressure. She wanted him, she wanted him so very much.

'Please...' Ellen began, but she needn't say more. Robert kissed her again, and this time, the pushing between her legs became firmer and much more insistent. There was a burn now, as her secret opening began to give way under his attention. Ellen shuddered, knowing what she must do. She spread her legs further apart, allowing him unreserved access.

Carring pushed hard once and breached her maidenhead in one smooth thrust. Ellen cried out in pain and shock. 'Oh!'

He plunged further, burying his cock to the hilt, until her body could take no more. Only then he stilled.

'Oh,' she moaned 'Oh, it is too much!' Ellen buried her face in his shoulder, pinned at the waist by the thick invasion between her legs.

'Shhh,' he soothed and kissed the top of her head, 'Shhh.'

Ellen opened her eyes and held Carring's gaze; desire and need blazed there.

'May I continue?' he asked, his voice strained.

The stretch and burn of his manhood imbedded so deep and wide within her made it almost impossible to speak, but she nodded.

He began to move, careful slick movements that took her breath away. The stretching discomfort lessened with each stroke, and at length, the same heavy womb sensation began to fill her again as her body accepted and began to relish his onslaught. He kissed her, sweetly on the lips, and she opened her mouth to his tongue. A low moan gathered in her throat as he moved more strongly within her. He growled, and pushed in hard before retracting, and thrusting hard again.

Her body began to grow tight, and her breathing matched his thrusts. She didn't know how her body could accept such pleasure, such intensity, but it did, and she adored it. Carring's movements became quicker, less smooth as he moved towards his own crisis. Ellen's hands curled around his neck as she clung to him, her back pushed hard against the wall, her sex growing ever tighter around his rigid manhood. A moment or two passed before her body broke with the same, wondrous pleasure it had earlier. She cried out into Carring's neck, and he bucked into her thrice more before shuddering and pumping his last.

Ellen could not say how long they clung to each other in the frantic final moments of passion, but after a time, the rainfall she'd forgotten about made itself known by falling heavier.

Mr Carring pulled away, his manhood slipped from between her legs, spilling his spent seed down her thigh as her skirts fell in a tumble. Her mind whirled, as she looked up and watched him pull up his breeches, and straighten his coat.

He held her gaze, but she could not read the thoughts that passed through.

A late carriage clattered past the alleyway, making her startle. 'I really must go,' she said softly and turned; an icy rivulet of rain trickled between her breasts. She felt hot and cold, thrilled but afraid.

Carring caught her hand. 'Tell me your name?' he asked.

She looked up into those beautiful eyes, relieved and perhaps vaguely saddened by the lack of recognition.

But he must never recognise me. She knew.

She had played a dangerous game this night, and one she must remember always, but *never* repeat.

'I cannot,' she said, 'goodnight.' Ellen pulled her hand free of his, and offered a polite curtsey.

'Please,' he called as she hurried out of the alley.

'Forgive me,' she said, as much to herself as to him, and then fled into night, just as the last lamps were extinguished.

Chapter 5

Ellen took a few false turns, to ensure Carring did not follow her back to Miss Brampton's, before finally returning to the school. She slipped in through the servants' quarters, for which she had a key, and rushed to her room, utterly terrified of discovery.

When she reached her small lodgings, she latched the door securely behind her. Her heart beat so fast and hard she thought it may burst.

The fire was nearly out; with trembling hands she placed some coal on the last of the embers.

She watched the flames grow and lick the black coal.

The evening had taken a dreamlike quality and she could scarce believe what she had done, yet her inner thighs were sticky and cold with Mr Carring's spendings, and her virginal blood evidence of what she'd done. Ellen bit her lip, and with a still shaking hand, she unbuttoned the gown and began to undress. As she struggled to lift the weighty dress over her head, her mind flashed with images of Mr Carring, licking her, sucking her, *there.* She'd never known a man would do such a thing, let alone contemplate it ever being done to *her.*

Oh! But it was wondrous. She wanted to laugh, perhaps even cry.

What was the correct response to these series of events? The novels she read never said.

Ellen lifted the gown off and lay it on the bed. She turned it and inspected it for damage or filth, and thankfully found nothing other than dampness from the rain. Her heart fluttered again with memories and she wondered if it would ever quiet. She half expected Mr or Mrs Sneddon to bang upon her door and inquire to her earlier whereabouts, but the schoolhouse was utterly silent except for the slow languorous chiming of the grandfather clock in the corridor.

Still not allowing a moment to reflect on the evening, Ellen lifted the dress and draped it over a chair. She brought out her dress brush, and brushed it down. Her strokes were methodical and purposeful. Just as Carring's sensual strokes had been.

Heat flushed up through her body and she dropped the brush to the floor and instead began to ready herself for slumber. Her hands were steadier as she unbuttoned her quilted stays, and lay them in her drawer. As she moved, she noticed increasingly tender sensations between her legs, every movement causing a slight twinge of discomfort and reminding her constantly of what she had done and the alarming size of the manhood with which she had done it.

Good grief!

Gingerly Ellen pulled up the skirts of her chemise, and moved towards her washbasin. Her inner thighs were streaked with his evidence of their passion.

She had a momentary pang of guilt and fear. If she ever were to marry, her husband would know what she had done. There would be no virginal blood on her wedding night as evidence of her chastity.

For I am no longer chaste.

She felt her belly twist.

But also, I am never to marry. She reminded herself, *I have been chosen as Miss Brampton's successor, and no married woman may be a schoolteacher.*

She nodded firmly to herself. No one would ever know of her indiscretion.

Her conscience mollified, she smiled slightly to herself and began to sponge away any evidence to the contrary.

What an adventure I've had!

***

Robert returned home in the early hours of the morning. The long chilly walk had done nothing to calm his mind, or sooth his arousal at the night he'd experienced.

It was extraordinary.

His ears echoed with the gentle sound of her moans, her cries of pleasure at her first experience of passion.

For all the thrills and excitement, he could not fathom why she had given her maidenhood away. Why had she not saved it for a husband? More curiously, why had she not asked for coin or anything else from him in return?

He had so many questions.

Who the devil was this wild, articulate woman? Where had she come from? Where had she gone?

Naturally, he'd tried to follow her as she wove around the streets, but she had proved elusive. He had lost her when a music hall had closed its doors and the last of its patrons had scattered along the street.

Robert sighed, and threw his coat down on the library chair. He stood before the roaring fire and spread his fingers wide to warm them. The heat of the fire reminded him of her hot thighs beneath his hands.

He groaned and ran his hands through his hair in frustration. He wanted to find the mystery woman more than he wanted anything else in his life.

There was a soft click of the door opening, and he turned as Potts entered. The butler looked dishevelled, as if roused from sleep. He carried a tray. The poor man appeared exhausted.

'A nightcap, sir?' he croaked, proffering a brandy and a slice of pound cake.

Robert smiled fondly. The man was worth his weight in gold. 'Thank you, dear Potts. Now I insist you retire, good evening,'

He glanced at the mantel clock, which read past midnight.

'You had a good walk, I take it?' Potts asked as he turned.

'Extraordinary,' Robert replied.

'Very good, sir,' Potts nodded and closed the door behind him.

Robert stepped forth and gulped the brandy, but it merely reminded him of the ale-laced breath of the woman at the public house, then he remembered her hot tight channel taking him to the hilt, the sweet tang of her taste and the sound of her moans.

Lord! He should never have let her go.

He tried to take his mind elsewhere, far from her curves, her heat, her passion; he stared into the coals. Not deterred, his mind swiftly returned to her.

Who was she? He asked again.

She was educated, certainly, and well-dressed obviously, but why would a woman of such calibre be out behaving in such a sensually scandalous manner? He could not fathom it. He had never met another woman who actually *had* desires, let alone the conviction to act on them, and that was frankly the most erotic thing he had ever encountered in his life.

Devil take him!

Why hadn't he chased her harder? Why hadn't he insisted she tell him who she was?

He had to find out.

His mind chased itself in circles over the same questions, as one glass of brandy turned into two, then two into three. Until, in the early hours of the morning, exhausted, Robert collapsed in his bed and finally found rest.

The next morning, Robert rose late, his stomach grumbling and his head pounding.

Just how many brandies had he consumed?

He glanced to his left; where weak winter sunlight cast a pale glow behind the curtains, his eyes ached.

His hand groped for the bellpull. He tugged and sank back into his pillows, rubbing his temples hard.

After a moment or two, Potts arrived with a tray of coffee and some morning cake. Robert peeled an eye open. Steam from the coffee coiled lazily in the frigid air, as Potts carefully set it down.

'Good morning, sir,' he said, and eyed the crumpled clothes strewn about the room. 'Sleep well?'

Robert groaned and he sat up, as Potts propped some pillows behind him.

'Devilish, I'm afraid. Devilish.'

Potts remained silent, and opened the curtains. Robert squinted in the light.

'Is Penny risen?' he asked groggily.

'Yes, sir, she's reading in the sunroom.' He could hear the disapproval in Potts voice.

Robert groaned guilty. 'Dress me and I'll join her.'

It took some time to coax his soaked bones from his bed, wash, and allow Potts to dress him. At length he went downstairs to breakfast with his daughter.

Guilt was heavy in his belly when he found, after he descended the stairs, Penny had already eaten and was taking tea.

His daughter looked a vision sitting by the window, her dark curls kissed by the weak London sunlight, and the vivid blue day gown complementing her rosy complexion. He was reminded savagely of his wife, Mildred. The guilt grew thicker.

He'd fornicated like the basest beast last night. Mildred would have been appalled.

And yet ... It had been a wondrous experience. Very wondrous indeed.

'Good morning, Daddy,' Penny rose and kissed his cheek lightly. 'Did you sleep well?'

He smiled and nodded, not prepared to contradict her.

The truth was shamefully lewd. He vaguely recalled lying awake in bed, soaked in brandy with an indefatigable erection. One would have thought after being sated for the first time since his wife's passing, he should have slept like dead. Alas, it was not until he'd relived each delicious moment of the evening, oiled his hand, given his cock a few hard strokes, and spilled seed across his belly that he'd finally found rest.

Colour threatened to bloom on his cheeks at the memory.

He coughed, and accepted a cup of tea proffered by Mrs Mathers. 'Penelope, I was thinking, to celebrate Christmas and your return home, we ought to decorate the house for the season,' he said. 'I know of several fine stalls down Hackney Road that offer holly, ivy and mistletoe for the festivities.'

He knew that there were stalls much closer to home that offered the same produce, but if he could perhaps take a walk about Hackney again, he may catch a glimpse of his elusive lady.

Penelope's eyes brightened, 'I could make pomanders!' she exclaimed, 'We must buy cloves and oranges. Oh, can we, Father?'

He beamed at her, 'Of course.'

So it was agreed. After a short delay during which he ate and supped on tea, they collected coats, bonnets and scarves to protect from the icy wind, and departed in their carriage to Hackney Road.

***

There was no luxurious lay-in or breakfast awaiting Ellen that morning, and she rose early. Her body was tender and her head more than a little achy. Her heart flip-flopped as she recalled the night's events.

Her body veritably cried out for his touch again.

Oh, Mr Carring!

Silly girl! she chided.

There was nothing for it, she had not the time nor temperament to linger on what was past, no matter how wickedly thrilling it was, or however much she wished to sit and reflect upon each forbidden detail.

There was, as always, work to be done.

She had to organise Mr Sneddon to return Miss Pickering's gown, sort the classrooms and prepare for the next school term, as per Miss Brampton's precise instructions.

She washed briskly in the washbasin. It was impossible not to relish the twinge of discomfort between her legs as a lingering, final reminder of Mr Carring's attention.

Last night, she had truly been free. She knew she was lucky to have experienced what she had. Most spinster schoolteachers had nothing more exciting in their lives than a student mispronouncing their Latin conjugated verbs. What she had experienced was a like a golden treasure. The passionate love of handsome man. Something she'd only dare dream of. Was it greedy to fantasise that Mr Carring could be hers, for not just one night but all the days and nights?

Oh, Mr Carring! Her heart fluttered as her disobliging mind returned to him. He was such a kind man, and good father. Not only that, but he had also been so concerned for her as a maiden—it was touching. She remembered how his head buried betwixt her thighs brought her such pleasure. Who even knew such a thing was done! Her body clenched. Though she told herself over and over it was just the one night and she should be thankful for that, she wished ardently there could be more.

Ridiculous, impossible!

Ellen pulled her brush through her hair, tearing at the knots.

She could never be anything more than Robert Carring's daughter's educator. No matter how much she wished it could be so.

If he ever did discover her true identity and indiscretion, her livelihood and reputation would be utterly destroyed.

Steeling her spine, Ellen slammed the brush down and pinned her mob-cap over her hair.

She was still chiding herself as she reached the lobby of the schoolhouse, where Mrs Sneddon busied herself polishing the skirtings.

'This mornin's porridge is cold, I'm afraid, Miss Smith, you're up late,' she added a little sourly, and looked up from her work. She paused and Ellen felt Mrs Sneddon's assessing gaze slide across her face. The deep creases in Mrs Sneddon's brow folded into deeper ones. 'You're looking very well this morning,' she said a little gruffly, her hand self-consciously patting her own mob-cap.

Ellen's heart stuttered, 'Am I? Thank you,' she replied, feeling a blush creep up her neck.

Mrs Sneddon hmphed and returned to her polishing.

'Is Mr Sneddon about? He needs to return this gown to the Pickerings,' she asked, her fingers stroking the fine fabric of the gown, remembering just how smooth it had felt as it had slipped over her skin, and how crudely it had been hitched to waist as Mr Carring...

Stop it! She warned herself.

'Mr Sneddon's out back, overseeing the coal delivery.' Mrs Sneddon said, her voice still gruff.

Ellen swallowed the thickness in her throat. 'Thank you.'

'And you'd best get that porridge into you, afore you start your day,' she added gruffly. 'Don't want ye gettin' sick while Miss Brampton's away, would we?'

'No, of course not,' Ellen agreed. She glanced towards the girls' classrooms, 'After my porridge, I shall go and buy more chalk for the classrooms. Some of the girls are down to very small stubs,' she said, then hesitated, knowing she must ask the next question. 'Is there anything at all you require from the shops or stalls, Mrs Sneddon?'

Mrs Sneddon stood, and brushed down her apron and smiled gratefully. 'As a matter of fact, Miss Smith, there is...'

***

Robert Carring meandered around the bustling stalls of Hackney Road, listening half-heartedly to the excited chatter of his daughter and absently handing over coin after coin as she purchased ivy, mistletoe, prickly, shiny holly and fruit to decorate their home. All the while, he searched for the golden-haired woman with her hair unbound. Though the streets were filled to capacity with vendors, beggars and businessmen, they were utterly devoid of the one for whom he searched.

And why would she be here? he reasoned, unable to stem his irritation. *Simply because she was here last evening does not mean she would be here now. She could be anywhere in London.*

'Come, Penny, I feel we have enough to decorate a palace, let alone our home,' he said, looking at the footman who carried the many bundles of greenery.

'Isn't it exciting?' Penelope exclaimed. Then laughed, 'Oh and look! There's Mr Sneddon, and what *is* he doing with Miss Pickering's dress? Oh, doesn't he look cross! I should never have expected to see such thing, he's usually so serious.'

Robert turned and saw the elderly butler from Miss Brampton's school, carefully lifting a stunning gown of brown and gold into a hack. He recognised the dress immediately. The glistening gold thread and the rich deep brown, the cut and style, it was unmistakable.

His shoulders grew taut. 'Whose dress, did you say?' he asked.

Penny glanced up at him, surprised by his poorly concealed interest. 'Why certainly that is Miss Pickering's gown, she wore it on our excursion to the orchestra.'

'Miss Pickering?' he asked slowly, as a low, uncomfortable sinking sensation grew in his belly.

'Why yes, Miss Pickering goes to Miss Brampton's as well, her family live over in Covent Garden. She can be devilishly naughty. Miss Smith chides her so when she laughs during hymn practice!' Penelope laughed at some memory. 'There was this time...'

Robert had stopped listening. A feeling of intense sickness swooped in his belly, and tightened his throat. *Oh please no.*

Robert remembered the feel of the fabric against his skin and cringed, her sudden cry on his entry. Had he ruined a girl, *his daughter's peer* last night? He prayed not.

Penelope continued, oblivious to his sudden quiet. 'She must have left it at the schoolhouse yesterday, I do recall her saying that her mother told her never to fold it in her luggage. She must have left it hanging and forgotten all about it. Poor Mr Sneddon, he does look more miserable than usual.'

Relief slipped down Robert's spine and he sighed gratefully. 'She returned home yesterday then?' he asked, trying to sound nonchalant.

'The day before, actually, her father came early as they have just welcomed a new baby into the family.'

'Thank goodness,' he breathed, he could simply have not lived with himself if he'd taken advantage of a young girl who knew no better.

Penelope looked quizzical, 'Yes, it is always a good thing when a baby arrives safely in the family, is it not? I should very much love a little brother or sister,' she said.

Robert looked at her seriously for a moment. Was his reticence to remarry depriving her?

He knew, in his heart, it was well past the time that he ought to have given his daughter a new mother and a sister, or brother, or two.

Robert looked down at her and nodded sagely, quite unable to respond.

They watched the elderly man organise himself in the hack. After a moment, he asked, 'Have all the staff and servants departed Miss Brampton's school?' he asked, his eyes travelling up the soot-blackened bricks, searching each heavily curtained window.

'Yes, only Mr and Mrs Sneddon are in residence, I believe,' she replied. 'It would be very lonely, I suppose, for them.'

Robert watched Mr Sneddon bark an address to the driver. Together, they watched the carriage pull away and down the street.

'And Miss Pickering's dress, where did she get it from?' Robert asked after a moment, 'it looks very fine.'

Penelope smiled broadly, 'Oh it is lovely, is it not? She has a very good tailor and she said she designed it herself.' She looked across at him slyly, 'Papa, are you thinking of getting me one such as that?'

Robert paused, wondering if perhaps he inquired to the dressmaker about a second gown, he may get closer to finding his mystery woman.

'Absolutely not,' he said, then added quickly, 'I should get you one in pink.'

Chapter 6

Loaded with enough goods to make a footman wince, Ellen made her way through the throngs of Christmas shoppers towards the school. Mrs Sneddon's shopping list had been extensive as it was expensive. Why Mr Sneddon could not have made these purchases and carried them back to the school in the hack was beyond her. Still, she *had* offered to shop, and so she really ought not complain, despite being nearly blinded by the volume of Mrs Sneddon's packages.

Glancing to her left, Ellen attempted to avoid a particularly damp and foul-looking puddle. As she did, she collided heavily into a fellow shopper on her right. Her packages wobbled precariously.

'Oh no!' she exclaimed, 'My chalk!'

As Ellen desperately tried to keep hold of the many, but less fragile packages for Mrs Sneddon, the dark brown paper parcel that contained fifty new sticks of chalk slipped from her bundle and crashed into the cobbles. She could hear them shatter.

'I'm terribly sorry!' a smooth gentleman's voice cried, and Ellen felt warm hands take her elbows to steady her. Surprised by the gentle contact, Ellen looked up, directly into the pale hazel eyes of Mr Carring.

For a time, she could not speak; heat as brutal as a strike of lightning lashed her cheeks. He stared down at her and for an indeterminable time, neither spoke. That was until Penelope Carring spoke for them.

'Miss Smith!' Penny exclaimed delightedly and swooped down to pick up the chalk package. 'I had no notion you were still at the school! What a surprise! Papa and I have been shopping for Christmas decorations! What have you got there?'

***

Robert's fingers tightened around the young schoolteacher's elbow as her face reddened in recognition.

'Forgive me, Mr Carring,' she murmured.

His eyes caught on her full lower lip as she bit down upon it and he felt a tug of familiarity. Her lips curled with a slight smile and she inclined her head politely at him then she turned to speak with Penelope. Though her demeanour had stiffened, her cheeks still burnt a painful crimson. Miss Smith responded gently to Penelope's chatter, but he heard nothing of what they said. Instead, his eyes scurried over Miss Smith. He had thought no one remained at the school but the Sneddons. He felt the tug of familiarity again. He studied her intently. Could *Miss Smith* be the woman? Was it possible that she had worn the dress last night and made merry in the pub? He cursed the dim lighting of the public house. If only he had had an opportunity to study his lover's face in better light, he could compare Miss Smith's for similarity.

Hot memories gripped him as he recalled his mystery lover, her heat and her passion. The wild mane of golden curls.

As his memories turned scorching, Carring's gaze reached the ridiculous mob-cap which covered the entirety of Miss Smith's scalp.

Dreadful things, mob-caps.

Certainly his passionate lover would not wear such an abomination?

Penelope's conversation quietened and his attention was drawn back to the present. He tried to get a better glance at Miss Smith's body, to compare it for the soft, gentle curves of the mystery woman.

In the sensibly thick and warm pelisse, he could not tell.

'I really ought to return to the school,' Miss Smith said, then looked at the sodden broken package in Penelope's hand, 'but I'm afraid I must return to the stationer, and purchase more chalk, these will certainly be ruined. I am dreadfully clumsy.'

Was this the voice of that same woman? He could not tell. Miss Smith's voice was soft, tremulous, a far cry from the certain, nay, demanding tones of his lover.

He sighed, uncertain and frustrated. Miss Smith certainly would have had the opportunity to try on the gown, but such behaviour was deeply out of character. True, there were similarities betwixt the two, height, and perhaps that blonde strand of hair escaping from the mob-cap, but, *no.* It must have been another woman, in a gown *like* Miss Pickering's who had caught his eye last night.

And yet...

'I insist on taking these parcels from you, Miss Smith,' Robert decided. 'And I shall replace your chalks. After all, it is I who walked into you and have caused their ruin...'

He saw Miss Smith swallow and she bit her lower lip again, this time the gesture sent a bolt of arousal straight to his groin. He felt his eyes narrow and considered her again.

She stammered something that could have been a refusal, but he slipped his hand from her elbow and began relieving her of her packages.

Her mouth fell open at his audaciousness, and he observed the neat rows of white teeth, and the hint of pink sweet tongue. The sense of familiarity grew.

'Mr Carring, really, the school is not far, I shall just drop these with Mrs

Sneddon and return to the stationer ... You really ought not inconvenience yourself.'

He ignored the protestations, 'It is of no inconvenience, Miss Smith, I assure you. It would be my pleasure.' He allowed the word to slide over his tongue.

Miss Smith's breath hitched, and beneath her heavy pelisse he saw her breasts rise and fall sharply. Her snapped her mouth closed, and her brows, almost completely covered by the lace of mob-cap, fell low.

He smiled.

She may not be his mystery lover, but there was certainly something about the young schoolteacher that made him wonder.

***

A real and sharp sense of excitement, bordering on panic, made the air difficult to breathe. Miss Smith coughed and inclined her head. 'If you insist, and it is not an inconvenience to Miss Carring?' she asked, offering a hopeful glance towards Penelope, who shook her head. 'Then stationer is this this way.'

Mr Carring fell into step beside her, his long legs taking slow considered steps to match her pace. Her heart thumped.

Good heavens, the man was even more dashing today than he was the night before.

More heat raced up her throat, her mind dashing back to those hectic, mad, sensuous moments in the alleyway.

Did he suspect her?'

Of course, he would not. Granted, only the lack of mob-cap and dim lighting had disguised her, Carring ought to have no reason to suspect her. Why, there were multiple ladies in London with whom she shared similar features.

'Miss Smith,' he began, 'How was your first evening of the holidays? Restful, I hope?'

Ellen glanced up sharply then away, so as to avoid his avidly studious gaze. Her throat was threatening to close and her mouth had turned so dry she could almost taste dust.

He does indeed suspect, she realised grimly.

She inhaled deeply, her mind racing with answers. Finally, she lifted her chin and gave a look as nonchalant as she could manage. 'Mr Carring, my employment as schoolmistress leaves little time for rest, I'm afraid.' She said sternly, 'Even though the students are returned home, there is much left to do. Why, Miss Brampton has left an extensive list of chores to be completed on her return. One does not like to disappoint Miss Brampton, I assure you. So no, Mr Carring, my evening was not particularly restful.'

Aha!

Ellen felt a small stirring of triumph. Ordinarily, she was a shamefully bad liar. Her mother had only needed to look her straight in the eye to know she told untruths. So, in general, she avoided lying outright. Exaggeration of minor truths and avoidance of direct questioning were skills she had honed since her early years.

She dared a glance up at Carring's eyes. Her heart skipped. His expression was searching and piercing. Her belly twisted with nerves. Perhaps the gentleman *was* clever enough to see through the veneer of her exaggerations.

Though his gaze remained studious, he made some understanding noises.

'And you, Mr Carring?' She asked knowing politeness required reciprocal questioning. 'Was your evening particularly restful?'

Much to her surprise, he laughed loudly, and she found herself staring. In his mirth, he threw his head back and chest swelled with amusement. 'Restful?' He chuckled. 'Restful it was not.'

Heat crept up her cheeks and she had to bite her lip to stem a smile. Of the many things their evening had been, she would most certainly agree, it had not been restful. Why, as they walked her sex ached with the memory of his heavy, hot manhood.

'I see,' she replied slowly as a sudden and dreadful desire to discover what he thought of their night together rushed to the forefront of her mind. 'And are you going to enlighten me to the cause of your restlessness? Or shall such a revelation remain secret?' Ellen asked, before she bit her tongue for her stupidity.

Had not a moment ago she inwardly crowed about her skills at exaggeration and avoidance? Then what had possessed her to ask this question?

Curse my impulsive heart!

She dared another glance, and found his pale hazel eyes studying her very, very intently. She swallowed and looked away towards the fast-approaching stationers.

'We are here!' Penelope called, racing towards the door to hold it open. 'Oh Papa, shall you buy me some paper so that I may write to cousin George? I have not returned his last letter, and it was very rude not to. Did you know he broke his leg? Did I tell you that? Well, he did. He was riding that big horse of his...'

Ellen moved towards the door so as to enter quickly. She felt, now more than ever, she was in very dangerous territory. She should not have asked that question. It was foolish, and it did not matter what he said in return. The sooner she departed his company the safer she would be. The more time she spent in his company, the more likely he was to recognise her.

Mr Carring moved quickly, 'I will see you inside, Penny,' he said, and gave his daughter a look so meaningful she stopped her chatter immediately, glanced betwixt her father and Ellen and hurried inside the door closing behind her.

Now, Carring's large body blocked entry to the store. Her gaze crawled up the length of his legs, to the impressive bulge in his breeches before slowly meeting his eyes.

'You asked me what made my night so restless.' He leant down closer to her, his breath brushed past her cheek. 'I am not a religious man, Miss Smith, but last night I was touched by an angel, who then so haunted my dreams, I scarce slept a wink.'

Her heart hiccupped. His mouth formed purposefully around the words. She watched avidly, for it was that same mouth, that same tongue that had delved between her thighs last night. She shivered.

'Do you know who that angel may be?' he drew even closer, and she could feel the heat radiate from him.

Ellen's heart thumped wildly. She needed to say something, anything that would withdraw his suspicions from her. For she was certain now he suspected the truth.

She stiffened her shoulders, 'It seems to me, Mr Carring, a rather thoughtless angel to disturb the sleep of men, even not-so religious men.' She twisted past him, pulling the door handle to open the shop door. She turned her head and looked over her shoulder, 'Perhaps you ought spend more time in church and God will send you a less selfish angel next time?'

Chapter 7

That evening, after Robert had returned Miss Smith and her packages to the school with a new, unbroken bundle of chalk, and decorated the house with an enthusiastic Penelope, he sat back in his library, swilling a glass of wine. Was Miss Ellen Smith his lover? Her comment of the angel suggested she knew something of the evening, but was it more likely she'd taken the notion in the literal sense.

Still, as he had leant down to speak with her outside the stationer's he'd tried to capture her scent, a hint of lavender perhaps? It was familiar. But then, how many young ladies used lavender? Many, he must admit.

Robert only half listened to Penelope as she chattered, pinning cloves into the oranges to make her pomanders. The scent was sweet, spicy and heady. He tried to imagine Miss Smith in Miss Pickering's beautiful dress, dancing and making merry. Though he had certainly seen evidence of spirit and definite intellect, he couldn't quite match the passionate woman with Miss Smith's upfront, and alarmingly moralistic banter, about church and God.

In fact, on their return walk to the school, Miss Smith had drawn him into an in-depth conversation on the Christian dogma and angelic visitation. She went so far as to enquire if his visitation hailed from the seraphim or cherubim. A question to which he could not possibly wittily respond.

No, though there were similarities, it was entirely unlikely Miss Smith of Miss Brampton's School for Ladies was his mystery lover. Perhaps it was time he investigated Miss Pickering's dress more thoroughly.

'Papa, what was it that you said to Miss Smith outside the stationer's shop today?' Penelope asked.

Drawn from his reverie, Robert's attention shifted to his daughter and her pomanders.

'I was speaking of ... angels,' he said after a moment.

'Oh, how dull. We hear enough of angels and saints at school. You're not going to start preaching to me, are you?' She gave him a worried glance.

'No, fear not Penelope, I shall not preach.'

'Good,' she sighed, placed down her pomander and yawned. 'Though I must say, you stared a lot at Miss Smith today, did you know? I think you made her nervous.'

Heat gathered on his cheeks. 'Did I?' he tried to be dismissive. 'I hadn't noticed.'

'You were. She is rather pretty, I suppose. I am so very surprised no one has married her.' She paused thoughtfully, 'Don't you think it a bit sad? A bit dull? Oh! Just imagine being a schoolteacher *forever!* I should rather die.'

***

Ellen was still giggling with mirth after she had her supper and retired for the night. Lying abed, she remembered the look on Carring's face when she'd asked him if his angelic visitation had been from the seraphim or cherubim. Usually so very refined, his jaw had dropped and he'd stared at her with such a look of perplexity that she'd nearly lost her composure and laughed out loud.

After all, what kind of angel was *she,* certainly no six-winged Angel from God's throne room. Actually, she was no kind of angel at all, or if she was, she was a certainly very unconventional one!

Oh, she was being naughty, silly, and playing with fire.

She could have very nearly been discovered today, she was very lucky indeed that she had not.

She rolled over and took a deep breath. Still, it had been so lovely to see him today. He was so very handsome, and it was exceedingly kind of him to buy her more chalk. Miss Brampton would have been furious that the first lot had been ruined, so really he was her angel today.

She rolled back over and faced the fire; the coals were dying, but her bed was warm. Though the day had been busy, exhausting even, she did not feel remotely tired. She felt a little excited.

A lot excited.

Down there.

She hissed and squeezed her legs tightly together. Far from sating her curiosity about carnal love, her night with Mr Carring had peeled open her imagination and made her desperate for more. Frustrated, she closed her eyes and squeezed her legs together tighter, relishing the faint ache that still lingered there. She could feel the beat of her heart, pulsing through every fibre of her being. She could feel the quilted nightdress, and the weight of blankets on every inch of her body. Ellen opened her eyes and rolled onto her back and stared at the ceiling.

Her hand slithered down the length of her body, knowing the destination before she herself did. As Mr Carring's hands had earlier, her own hands pulled up the fabric of her nightdress, bunching it at her waist. She had to get rid of this crazed carnality that was plaguing her, perhaps easing the pulsing, driving heat between her legs would return her body to its usual calm state.

Or perhaps it would make it even worse.

It could not. It was not possible to feel wilder, or more lusty, than she did now.

Working nearly of their own accord, Ellen's fingers swept through the curls that covered her sex. They moved swiftly, seeking the wet flesh so recently tended by Mr Carring.

Her body jerked as her middle finger slipped between the folds of her womanhood. She moved the finger up, around and over the hard bead of pleasure before slipping back down and pressing into her hot channel. She flinched and her knees opened wider as she repeated the rhythm over and over.

As her finger slipped and danced over delicate flesh, Ellen remembered Mr Carring's tongue doing that very same dance. Pleasure coiled low in her body as she recalled the roughness of his cheeks on her soft inner thighs, the sweet decadence of his hot tongue as it licked the same path her finger now travelled.

Ellen moaned at the memory and pushed her finger deep into her sex before retracting it and sweeping it over the hard pearl. She remembered the hard length of his manhood pushing into her and stretching her tight unused flesh, the taste of his lips on her hers. She whimpered, and her fingers moved faster. Finally she recalled the powerful bucks of Mr Carring's hips as he met with crisis, thrusting so deep into her she thought her body might break with pleasure. Her body clenched and sweetness broke over her as her sensitive sex could no longer take the ministrations of her fingers nor the memories in her mind. She cried out, thrusting her head back into the pillow as her channel clenched longingly around her finger.

After a time, she slipped her hand away and pulled her nightdress down. Her body throbbed with remnant pleasure and her heart beat rapidly. She rolled over and gazed into the smouldering coal embers, her eyes half closed, and sighed.

Chapter 8

Why could he simply not forget about it? Why did he have to moon and dream of seeing her again? There were plenty of other women in London, probably slightly more chaste as well. Yet he didn't want one of those women, he never had. He wanted his mystery woman, a woman who had gone out and given herself the Christmas gift of freedom. A daring woman, a strong woman, a woman with conviction.

And what about Miss Smith?

She, like his mystery woman, had remained something of an enigma, drifting into his thoughts and dreams when he least expected it.

After meeting her at the stationer, he wasn't entirely convinced she was not the mystery woman. Though her clever talk of angels and Christian theology made him doubtful, the juicy lobe of her lip and the sweet curves of a womanly body beneath her pelisse gave him pause.

Still, he had decided to follow the lead of Miss Pickering's dress. If there were other dresses like it about London, then the chance that Miss Smith was his mystery lover would be lower.

Frustratingly, it had taken the entire week to get an appointment with Miss Pickering's dressmaker, and he had high hopes the lady of the establishment may know something of a replica dress that may point him in the right direction of his lover.

Miss Pickering's dressmaker was Howell's, a very fine establishment, and upon entry, he realised exactly why it had taken a week to get the appointment. The gowns on display were exquisite. The rolls of fabric rich, bright and expensive.

To keep his investigation secret from his daughter, he had come under the ruse of having Penelope fitted for a new winter gown.

He sat taking tea with the lady of the establishment, Mrs Harcourt, whilst a seamstress took Penelope for measurement. Mrs Harcourt was a tall grey-haired woman, who was as graceful as she was stern.

'Have you a particular design in mind for your daughter, Mr Carring?

She has a fine figure and a perfect complexion,' she asked, and gestured to a book of dress designs on the table. 'You may peruse those, they are this season's newest and I suspect would suit her best.'

'Thank you,' Robert said, and took the book. It was weighty and thick.

Carefully he flicked through a few pages. The sketches of the gowns were well executed and brightly colourful. He paused on the page of a rather ostentatious pink and green spring gown.

She raised an eyebrow at his choice. He coughed and turned the page, but dismissed the next golden yellow and blue dress. 'My daughter tells me you made a lovely brown and gold gown for Miss Pickering earlier this year? May I see that design?' he asked.

Mrs Harcourt looked up from the design on the open page and paused thoughtfully, 'Oh yes, I recall it,' she nodded. 'If I am not mistaken, Miss Pickering has a talent for dress design and she drew the pattern herself. We were only too happy to make it for her.

You will not find its like in our design book, however.'

Hope swelled in his chest. 'And have you used the design since?'

Mrs Harcourt looked away and patted her mob-cap as if assessing it for loose strands. 'Only once, and with Miss Pickering's approval of course,' she added hastily. 'It was for a lady who has a haberdashery shop on Fleet Street.'

Robert's heart thumped. 'Do you happen to recall that lady's name?'

'Of course, I purchase many of our fabrics from her, it's Mrs Debenham.'

Robert felt his heart thump with nerves. There was a chance that Miss Smith was not his lover. He wasn't sure how that made him feel.

It certainly opened up many questions.

Perhaps the other woman with the dress was married? Had she come to Hackney Road to experience some excitement away from the confines of her marital home?

He paused, no, that could not be. His lady had been a virgin, he remembered the tightness of her sheath around his cock, milking him quickly to completion.

Heat crawled up his neck at the memory.

He coughed, trying to cover the increasing lewdness of his thoughts. 'I think I may know the lady, is she a blonde, youthful, well-bred sort?' he asked.

Mrs Harcourt tittered behind her hand. 'I don't know to which Mrs Debenham you are referring, but my Mrs Debenham is just shy of fifty and nine and as grey as a goose.'

Robert recalled the plump fullness of his lover, and the youthful spring in her step.

'Most definitely not the lady to whom I refer, then.'

***

That same evening, Ellen found herself supping alone. The Sneddons had been called away. Mrs Sneddon's sister had fallen abruptly ill and they had rushed to her side; if all was well, they would return in a day or two. Initially, Ellen had been secretly delighted by their absence but soon the silence of the schoolhouse was all encompassing. The clock ticked obnoxiously loudly, and the coals crackled in the fireplace, taunting her with their own merriment. The minutes seemed to crawl past, unwilling or unable to go any faster. Ellen thought she may go mad.

She constantly chided herself. She ought not be so ungrateful. She was warm, Mr Sneddon had kindly left ample coal for her to restoke the fires. Her belly comfortably full, Mrs Sneddon had left two suppers and cold porridge so that she would not starve. Perhaps less kindly, Mrs Sneddon had also left a list of multiple chores to keep her busy.

Alas, without the distraction of cups of tea and conversation, Ellen had completed most of the chores by midmorning, leaving some for the following day, lest the boredom became too great. Thus, since luncheon, there had been precious little for her to do but take tea, sew or read. All of which she'd spent hours doing, and now with the sun setting so early, the prospect of a long dark evening seemed incredibly depressing. Worst of all, she couldn't stop thinking of Mr Carring. The tedium made her mind fractious, constantly drawn to him, to his touch, to the memory of his manly affections.

Ellen had thought she'd be relieved when Miss Pickering's gown was returned, for in its absence, her desire to wander the streets of London seducing gentlemen had dissipated. But a mortifying realisation had quickly followed. The *only* man in London she wished to seduce again was Mr Carring and as she had told herself many, many times, doing that again was out of the question. Her wild, extravagant night with Mr Carring was swiftly turning into a delicious dream, a wonderful Christmas treat that she could always, and *only,* revisit in memories.

But...

Ellen stood in a swish of skirts and stalked to the window, pulling open the thick curtains. Her breath instantly fogged the window as she gazed out over the street.

Oh, how she wished she could have another night like that. Another night with *him.* For it was not just the act, the freedom or impropriety that had thrilled her, but the man with whom she'd done it all. He was passionate, considerate, kind—everything she could ever have wished to find in a gentleman.

She pressed her hot forehead against the cold smooth glass. Did he think of her? Miss Smith, schoolteacher, or did he think of her only as the lusty, wild woman? She remembered the intensity of his gaze at the stationers, the searching looking as he wondered who exactly she was.

Had she just been a fun dalliance? Did he make a habit of sating himself on willing women outside public houses? She frowned and pressed her forehead harder into the glass. The very thought of him finding another, or worse, marrying another woman made her feel hot and cold and torn with confusion.

It should not, but it did.

She had no claim on the gentleman, no matter how much she wished to.

No, she needed to gather her wits and common sense. After all, she *would* see him again. Albeit not in the way she would like. He could not see her as the sultry wanton he'd worshipped with his tongue in that alley way, but as a very proper schoolmistress, and when he did, Ellen had absolutely no idea how she could behave. She'd have to be calm, collected, indifferent even. If she gave anything away he would quickly discover the truth; why, he almost had the other day.

Ellen opened her eyes and looked down at the street, she could hear carollers singing outside, or perhaps they were patrons of the public house spreading some Christmas cheer. She looked up the street and saw them, dressed warmly for the cold. A tall gentleman threw his head back and laughed, his voice booming through the wintery air.

Her skin prickled.

She wanted desperately to join them. She wanted to laugh and sing too. Walk around the streets spreading cheer.

She glanced at the clock on the mantel. It was five o'clock, she could go and sing for an hour or so before retiring for the night. Singing wasn't a wicked or wanton thing to do. The carollers were probably part of the church choir. There was naught wrong with joining them for just an hour or so. At the very least it would get Mr Carring from her mind and some Christmas cheer would do her good.

She was decided. Quickly she ran upstairs to grab her pelisse and a warm winter bonnet. She pulled off her mob-cap, freeing the riots of golden curls before tying the neat grey ribbon beneath her chin, finally she pulled off her slippers and laced up her boots, then hurried out the servants' entrance.

However, when Ellen reached the street, the carollers were nowhere to be seen. She'd taken too long lacing her boots and tying her bonnet.

If she'd been a lesser woman, she may have cursed her rotten luck.

She looked around. A few stalls selling candles and Christmas decorations remained, the vendors hunched in greatcoats and hats, hiding from the wind that suddenly gusted. She strained her ears over the bustle of carriages and the chatter of salesmen, but she could not hear the carollers. She felt herself frown.

Still, not to be disheartened, she strode up the street towards the teashop. Perhaps the singers had headed there and were getting a warm brew to wet their throats before continuing.

She hurried past a family browsing the remaining stalls, and up to the teashop.

Instead of the usual warm lamps and the murmur of chatter, the teashop was closed, a sign on the door indicating they'd not open until two days hence.

Ellen shivered. It had been a silly idea to join the carollers. She stopped and paused, realising exactly where she was.

The alleyway was to her left.

Memories rushed around her. The sounds of their carnal passion, the cold of the wet bricks on her back.

She bit her lip and stared into its gloomy depths, her breath catching in her throat.

Chapter 9

Robert Carring knew it was her immediately.

Late in the evenings, usually after supper and Penelope had retired for the night, he came to the public house in Hackney in the hope she'd return.

And return she had.

This evening, when Robert stepped out of the smoky warmth of the pub he'd noticed a woman, her head covered with a modest grey bonnet. Beneath the bonnet, unbound golden curls swayed in the wind. She was staring down the alleyway. Even in the lamplight he could see the familiar tilt of her chin, and the curve of a well-formed lip. He recognised her immediately.

'Miss Smith,' he called. For all her clever talk of cherubim and seraphim, she must be his lover. What other reason could there be for her being here? The sense of familiarity was overwhelming.

His voice carried well in the cold air, and she stiffened immediately. She turned, her pelisse and skirts wrapping around her legs.

Large eyes widened, dark colour roared up pale cheeks, and her mouth fell open.

He knew in his heart it could be no coincidence that Miss Smith was here, staring down the alley where they had been so intimate.

But if he were wrong...

The thought paralysed him.

If, through some mighty error in his understanding of circumstance, Miss Smith was not the woman he had deflowered in the alley—what possible lie could he concoct to explain his presence now or his questioning of her?

There was no lie. He *had* to be right.

His heart pounded in his ears at the prospect of confronting her with his suspicion. If he left now, no one would be the wiser. He need not embarrass himself, he could disappear back home and never think of it again.

No, that simply was not good enough.

He had been traipsing about London nearly every night in search for her, and now he'd found her. His blood warmed with excitement. He wanted to taste that vivacious zest for life, and her raw uncensored passion. If Miss Smith was indeed that woman, then he simply had to let her know and hope that his own feelings were returned.

'Miss Smith?' There was silence; it seemed at that moment that not a soul in London existed but them.

'Mr Carring?' Her voice carried through the frigid air, soft, incredulous, but undoubtedly the voice of the woman for whom he had so ardently searched. 'What are you...'

But Lord! How could he ever have mistaken her?

Elation filled his chest. He needed to hear her say it.

'Tell me it was you,' he demanded breathlessly.

***

Ellen's head pounded. The sound of her own blood roared in her ears.

She stared at Mr Carring. He stood proud, tall, and strong.

She'd been discovered.

It was terrifying, it was exhilarating.

But the cold reality would likely be humiliating.

Unthinkingly, Ellen ran a hand through a knot of hair that had tangled in the wind. The hand shook. Mr Carring stared at her, waiting for her answer. His broad shoulders tense and his expression unreadable.

He will expose me. The realisation ran through her head.

She had been so foolish to speak of angels earlier, she should have made other excuses, been more vague, been...

'Miss Smith, I insist we speak immediately,' Carring demanded.

What was the sound in his voice? Outrage? Anger? At this distance, she couldn't quite discern.

'Really, this is not appropriate, sir, I have ... I have ... no chaperone,' her voice shook, and a few slow lazy snowflakes began to fall from the sky.

He barked a laugh. 'You had no chaperone last week,' he declared. 'Yet that certainly did not stop you.'

Nausea boiled in her body. Would he make a scene if she tried to dismiss him? 'Please, Mr Carring...' She implored. If he was any sort of gentleman he'd let her go, forget what had happened. 'I know nothing of what you speak,' she said.

He laughed again and stepped closer; she could smell his cologne, and its scent was evocative. His hand moved and captured hers.

Even through the leather of gloves, she could feel his heat.

'Come now, you must think me a fool.' His words were silky and he was so close now she could see his lips curl with the slightest smile. She remembered the feel of them against her skin.

She swallowed. 'No,' she stammered. 'I could never think you a fool.'

'Then what exactly do you think, Miss Smith? I simply must know.'

'I cannot say,' She answered.

Ellen bit her lip hard, was he playing some cruel game with her? She knew at any moment he could rail at her, call her a whore, and insist upon her dismissal from the school. It was expected.

The hair on her neck curled as she glanced up and down the street, praying no one was eavesdropping on their intense, strange intercourse.

She shivered.

'How rude of me,' Carring exclaimed, 'Come into the public house, we can discuss matters there, or I could walk you back to the school, if you would prefer?' he said, as if noticing the cold for the first time.

She straightened, 'No, not the school,' she whispered.

'Then the public house it is,' his tone was firm.

Her stomach fluttered, then twisted. To return to the scene of her debauchery had been foolish.

The snow had begun to fall in earnest and a flurry of snow swept into the entrance of the pub as they opened the door. His hand gripped her elbow as he steered her into the smoky pub. The grip was not tight, but she felt it acutely.

The poor lighting made him seem larger, fiercer. His eyes glittered with a silent appraisal that she couldn't quite decipher.

She her body felt torn; in part, the situation was thrilling, but also very frightening. She may very well lose everything this night.

The public house's dim smoky warmth embraced them as Carring drew her to a quiet nook table and gestured her to sit. 'Do you wish for refreshment?' he asked.

Ellen watched his mouth move and swallowed.

She ought to say no, offer some modicum of ladylike decorum, but ale would be very welcome, if only to settle her trembling hands.

'Ale, thank you,' she said after a pause.

He nodded, that cryptic smile playing on the corner of his lips again.

Her heart thudded.

'Do not go anywhere,' he said, his voice soft but stern. 'I have been coming near here every evening searching for you, I do not want to be disappointed.'

Ellen swallowed, and watched him walk through the tables towards the bar.

He'd been searching for her? Why? Was that what most gentlemen did after a liaison with a woman? She thought it most unlikely.

She watched him speak with the publican and order their drinks. He made a few gestures and the publican handed over the drinks and a small key.

She frowned.

'The frown does not suit you, Miss Smith,' he said as he deposited a tankard of ale before her and slipped the key in his pocket.

Ellen gripped the cool tankard and gulped to steady her nerves.

'But now you must tell me. It *was* you, was it not?' He asked, and swept down into the nook beside her.

The snow had turned to crystalline droplets on his coat, they shimmered in the poor light of the pub.

She lifted her gaze to his.

She had to be clever about this, admit nothing until she knew his intentions.

She inhaled deeply. 'If, through some extraordinary circumstance, I knew of what you spoke, what would you say?'

He smiled broadly now, his teeth glittering white. 'Oh but you are so clever, Miss Smith, I do so like fine wit and intelligence in a woman. Your speak of angels nearly had me fooled.'

Her cheeks burnt but she wanted to laugh.

'Oh, your angelic visitation? Is this to what you refer?' she pressed, feigning ignorance.

He laughed softly under his breath and took a gulp of his own ale. 'Yes, and I cannot tell you how ardently I wish for another.'

His gaze was heavy, Ellen swallowed.

'And if you were so blessed with another visitation, what is it that you would say to this angel? Would you rail at her for leaving her lofty heights?' Her voice shook, 'Would you tell her superiors how far she has fallen?' she asked, her voice throaty.

Carring's hand slipped over the table and curled around her own.

'I would say that she need not fear me. I would never disclose her secrets to anyone. I would say that I am haunted by her vision and that our one night together is not enough.'

Ellen's chest heaved, relief ran like water through her veins.

Her shoulders softened at the admission.

Carring continued, 'I would offer that angel another, or as many nights of freedom as she wished.' he breathed, 'Because one night will never be enough, will it, Miss Smith?'

'No,' she breathed. 'Never enough...'

Chapter 10

He wanted to kiss her, he wanted to make love to her. The key in his pocket felt heavy and disused.

Finally she had admitted it.

His lover was Miss Smith.

The murmur of the public house became unbearably loud, and the presence of so many people crushing.

'Will you come upstairs with me? I have a room to which we can go,' the words came out all tumbled. 'Perhaps we can speak more plainly there?'

He watched Ellen bite her plump lip again and his cock surged in his breeches. He was being too forward, he'd frighten her away.

'Yes,' she replied without preamble. 'I will, but you must promise me, you will never speak of this to Miss Brampton, or anyone.'

He smiled. 'Have I not already made that promise?'

'You have, but I must hear it.' She looked so serious.

Robert nodded. 'I, Robert Carring, will never disclose our secret to anyone. Miss Smith may trust me implicitly.'

She nodded then added with a mischievous smile. 'Then let us go upstairs, Mr Carring—but let us not talk. I feel we have spoken quite enough.'

Her words set his heart pounding and he was in no need of further encouragement. He caught the eye of the barman and nodded. Gently, he took hold of Miss Smith's hand and led her through the tables of patrons towards the wooden stairwell at the rear of the public house. Most pubs offered lodgings, and even if Miss Smith had declined his offer he'd probably have stayed the night, for the snow was falling heavier outside.

None of the other patrons so much as cast an eye their way as the gentleman and his lady ascended the stairs to the lodging rooms.

A sense of thrilling anticipation rushed through his body as Robert unlocked the first door on their left with the key from his pocket. A small, clean room opened up before them. It smelled slightly smoky, and there was a small new fire in the hearth, just enough to keep the ice from the air. The curtains were drawn, and a small double bed with thick green quilts rested beside the far wall. Its plump pillows were inviting.

He felt Miss Smith hesitate and just for a moment, he feared she may baulk and leave. He turned to her, expecting to see a face drawn with worry or angst. Yet when he looked down at her pretty face, he found her eyes bright with excitement.

'I have never stayed in a public house,' she breathed and stepped into the room, she spun on her heel, sending the skirt of her long pelisse flying.

He closed and latched the door, and as he turned, he saw her continue her wild spinning.

Robert felt himself laugh and he reached out to capture her in his arms, her excitement infectious. She succumbed to his embrace readily.

Robert looked down at her glowing cheeks and kissed her.

She was as sweet as he remembered, her mouth parted eagerly for his and her small tongue reached out exploring. Such passion he'd never known in a woman.

Sensations swamped him. 'Miss Smith,' he moaned and kissed her harder.

She groaned softly in response and pressed her body to his. Even through the layers of his jacket and her pelisse, he could feel her breasts crush against his chest.

'Take this off,' he growled and moved his kisses to her cheek, then her neck, 'No bonnet, no coats, no dresses. Just you, Miss Smith. I must have *just you.*'

Miss Smith pulled away and looked up, holding his gaze steadily. Her cheeks were flushed with pleasure. 'Ellen, my name is Ellen,' she said, and began to undo the ribbons beneath her chin.

After just a short time, she pulled the bonnet from her head. Robert's cock grew harder as her golden curls burst eagerly from their confinement. Would her breasts do the same? he wondered.

Her lips curled in a naughty smile, as if she'd read his thoughts. Her small hands moved towards the buttons of her pelisse and began to undo them, one by one, her eyes never leaving his.

Soon her pelisse tumbled to the ground, and her small hands began to work at the buttons of her matronly schoolmarm's gown. That too was shortly discarded, and she stood before him in nothing but her shift, quilted stays and stockings.

Robert studied her. He was surprised and aroused by how her body appeared so vulnerable yet her eyes were wild with excitement and passion.

'Mr Carring,' she said as her hands moved towards the laces of her stays. 'What are you thinking?' Her fingers toyed with the long thin laces coquettishly.

Robert swallowed, 'What I am thinking is entirely too vulgar to say,' he said and moved towards the bed, where he sat and pulled off his boots and jacket.

When he looked up, Ellen was smiling again. She pulled the stays loose before lowering them to the floor.

Robert gazed at her, without the stays, he could see her nipples harden through her shift. He swallowed as her lips curled in a broader, knowing smile.

It was hard to accept that this passionate vixen was the very same woman who tutored his daughter so artfully.

Not waiting, Robert unbuttoned his waistcoat and flung it away. As he did, Ellen bent to the hems of her skirt and lifted the entire thing from her body.

Speech was denied him as she stood before him, naked except for her stockings and winter boots. His eyes travelled from her glittering eyes, down the fine line of her throat and lingered at the heavy swell of her breasts. They were beautiful, blue-veined and full, his mouth watered to suckle them. Yet greedily, his eyes travelled over the round soft belly to the juncture of her thighs. Light brown curls hid the lush, tight sex there. He groaned and beckoned her to the bed.

She came towards him, her hips sashaying left and right. Soon she stood before him, and her hands moved to the buttons of his shirt. 'It only seems fair that you also remove your clothing,' she murmured, then gasped as he leant forward and captured one of her rosy nipples in his mouth. Her hands faltered on his buttons, and she threw her head back and moaned. Robert drew the nipple deep into his mouth, tasting her sweetness and relishing the impossible softness of her. Then he released her.

She cried out and looked down at him, her eyes blazing with need. Her hands worked faster at the buttons and quickly it too lay discarded on the floor. Now Robert stood, and pushed her gently back onto the bed, her nipples hard and erect. He unlaced her boots and rested them on the floor. She lay back, waiting, as finally, he removed his breeches.

***

Ellen had never seen a man in his naked glory. Her breath left her as she avidly gazed at Carring's superbly masculine form. His chest was broad and sculpted, with just the finest dusting of dark hair. She let her gaze wander down past the ridges of abdominal muscles and narrow waist to that which she had been dreaming about. His cock was hard, and stood rigidly to attention. It was enormous.

Her sex pulsed with need. Would it hurt as it had the last time? She doubted it, and that pain hadn't lasted long.

Her thoughts were cut short as the bed sunk under his weight. He moved between her legs, opening them wide as if for assessment.

'I have dreamed of seeing this,' he said, his voice guttural. 'My wife ... she never ... I never was able to...' His words failed, and Ellen let her legs fall wide, exposing her most intimate parts to Carring's devouring gaze.

'You are like an exotic flower,' he moaned, and lowered his head between her thighs. She felt his tongue, hot and wet, slip between the lips of womanhood and test her channel. She moaned, rolling her hips high to try and get more of him. His tongue flickered out and around her pearl before delving in again. 'Your nectar is my opium,' he murmured, his words half lost. He pressed his face further into her, so that she could feel the stubble of his chin graze against her skin.

She cried out, her hands reaching down and curling in his hair. 'More,' she whispered, 'I need more.' Her heart felt as if it may run away, and her body scorched with heat.

Carring obliged her, at her bidding he moved his face from her sex and positioned himself above her, the hot head of his cock nudging at the slick, hungry entrance of her tunnel.

So rapt in pleasure, Ellen had no time to brace herself for his entry. She felt him surge forward, pushing into her hard and deep.

Ellen cried out, her eyes flying open. Cradled in between his arms, she looked up into his face. Roberts handsome face was taut, and his pupils dilated with need. He leant down and kissed her tenderly.

After a few kisses, Ellen felt her womanhood grow accustomed to his girth, the momentary discomfort fading to nothing but sweet pleasurable pressure. Then he began to move. He thrust his hot length into her, then withdrew, only to plunge back and repeat the process.

Ellen grew insensible, she was no longer Miss Ellen Smith, schoolteacher, but a vessel of pleasure. Every inch of her body was alive and full of sensation, from the deep stretched flesh of sex to the tips of her nipples that grazed Carring's hard muscular chest with every thrust.

They may have stayed in that erotic dance moments, hours or years and Ellen wouldn't have known the difference—so consumed with need and pleasure. When finally, the thumping of Carring's manhood deep in her womanhood sparked a newer, more intense sweetness, she groaned, opening her legs wider to give him deeper access.

'Please don't stop,' she cried, and curled her arms around his neck to draw him closer. They kissed as he pumped harder into her. The stretch and release, and relentless pulsing, became everything, until, like a rainstorm, sweet powerful pleasure broke within her.

Ellen cried and wrapped her legs around his waist, pulling him ever deeper into her body. 'Carring,' she moaned as wave upon wave of pleasure made her sex clench around him. Then she felt it, a spasm roared up the length of his cock and hot seed spilled into her over, and over again. She held him to her tightly until the last of their crisis ended.

***

Robert felt Ellen's legs fall open, releasing him from their carnal hold. He could feel the mad pounding of her heart through her breasts crushed hard against his chest. She stirred beneath him, and Carring watched her pretty eyes open.

'Are you well?' he asked. 'I did not hurt you?'

That naughty smile curled her lips, 'Far from it, Mr Carring. You gave me yet another Christmas gift to treasure.'

He returned the smile, and lifted himself away. His cock slipped from her and he sat up, glancing down at juncture of her thighs. The blonde curls of her womanhood had parted, displaying her glittering, pink sex, open and still inviting. His pearly seed glistened at the mouth of her channel.

His cock stirred again at the sight. He had never seen anything so flagrantly erotic.

He looked up, and found Ellen watching him. He expected her to snap her legs closed at his lewd gaze, yet she did not. Her eyes sparkled, and she snaked a hand down the length of her body. It trailed over her belly and slipped past the curls between her open legs. Her fingers traced the dark pink inner lips of her sex and slipped in the copious seed.

His cock reared up against his thigh, 'You are exquisite,' he growled.

Ellen released a throaty laugh, and her hand left her body as she pulled him back atop her. 'As are you, Mr Carring,' she whispered and kissed his ear. His cock was hard again, desperate to taste her again. He felt her legs widen once more. With no effort at all, he slipped his throbbing cock back home. It slipped in smoothly, its passage eased by the volume of his spent seed.

Once more they began their sensual dance, though this time it was slower, slicker, and more considered.

Much later, they lay together covered in the green quilts; the fire had died from neglect and the air in the room chilly. Many hours had passed, as they'd talked, kissed and made love.

'I have never known a woman to enjoy intimacy as you do. It pleases me.' Carring said, coiling one of her golden curls around his finger.

She looked at him and raised an artful brow. 'No?' She smiled, 'But what of your wife? How is it she could not enjoy your bounty?'

He chuckled, 'My wife did not enjoy our relations, she endured them.'

Ellen was quiet. 'I find that impossible to believe.'

He snorted, 'Our marriage was arranged, and my parents thought us a good match. She was pretty, well read and clever, but she had no passion for me.'

Ellen's finger traced a line around the muscles of his chest. 'How extraordinary. Forgive me for saying so, but she can't have been that clever. For I have always found you exceedingly charming.'

Robert laughed and kissed her forehead.

She reciprocated his smile, but it shortly faded.

'I really must return to the school,' the sun was rising through the smog. 'The Sneddons are away, but I am uncertain when they will return. It would not do to have them return and find me absent. I cannot risk my position any more than I already have...' She paused and held his gaze. 'I am sure you understand?'

He studied her, suddenly feeling conflicted, and guilty for having held her here so long. 'I do,' he agreed. 'I will walk you there.'

She sat up. 'No, I do not think that would be wise. We ought not be seen together. London is a crowded place, but we ought not tempt fate.' She paused, 'But thank you, for your discretion and...' she gestured to the bed, rumpled by their lovemaking. 'This. I had never thought to experience such things and I am truly grateful.'

Robert felt his brow furrow. 'What are you saying, Ellen? That we ought not meet again?'

He saw her throat contract as she swallowed. 'It is dangerous for me, I should not make a habit of...'

His frown deepened. 'Make a habit of what?'

She slipped from the bed, and he watched her plump, round derriere move towards the previously discarded shift. She did not answer.

A sense of alarm filled him, was she saying she would never see him again? The notion filled him with ire. It was unacceptable.

'Make a habit of what? Meeting me? Or meeting other men?'

He regretted his last angry words immediately.

Ellen pulled the shift over her head. 'Do not be ridiculous.' Her eyes flared. 'There has never been anyone but you, and there shall not be.'

He looked away as she bent to pick up her stays. 'Forgive me, I did not mean that.'

He stood to assist her with lacing. She made a noise of displeasure, but allowed him to lace the contraption.

'You must understand, I have a position to uphold, Mr Carring.'

'Robert,' he corrected.

'Robert.'

His name slipped from her lips like liquid.

'I very much like my dalliances with you...' she began.

Dalliances? Was that all they were?

'But I cannot risk my livelihood and reputation. And nor should you.'

He sighed and picked up her dress and handed it to her. She was right.

'You are a man of position and wealth, it would not do to cause scandal. If not for you, then Penelope. As for me, I am a teacher, and my very reputation depends on your discretion ... and in truth, I find it very difficult to be discreet with you. Why, just look at this evening...' she began. 'How many in this street may recognise me? Goodness, I have been so foolish.'

Robert jaw tightened with sudden frustration. He pulled on his breeches. Gooseflesh rippled over his skin. He caught Ellen staring at his chest, a look of distinct longing in her gaze.

For a time, he said nothing. He wanted to argue. He wanted to contradict her and say that all was well, that they could continue in this fashion for eternity if she wished. Yet he knew they should not. He cared not for his own reputation but was shocked to realise he did care very much for hers.

'You are, of course, right,' he agreed after a moment. Discretion was vital, and thus far they had not been at all that discreet.

Such indiscretions could cause Ellen untold harm, and that was unacceptable.

'Ellen...' he began, 'Perhaps it is for the best that we do not do this again.'

A look of acute displeasure rushed over her pretty face as she shrugged her pelisse over her dress, but she smoothed it away. 'Yes, it is probably for the best.'

Chapter 11

Two days had passed since the glorious night in the public house, and Ellen was feeling thoroughly depressed. Her heart and body yearned to see Carring again. She longed to have more lazy conversations in bed like they had that night in that chilly public lodging room. She longed to make love again.

It was ridiculous and preposterous.

It could not happen again.

She'd been lucky on both occasions that no one had recognised her. She ought not to tempt fate.

Thus she had busied herself as much as possible in the school. The Sneddons had sent word that they would remain with Mrs Sneddon's sister a few days longer, so the days in the empty schoolhouse were interminable.

She relived her moments with Robert over and over in her head, and she spent inordinate hours staring out the windows over Hackney Road trying to see if he had returned for her.

It was pointless, for he would not, she knew. She had asked him not to, and he had promised his discretion.

She stood and shovelled more coal into the fireplace and warmed her hands. She'd had to go out to the market today and purchase food. As she'd walked about the stalls, she tried to spy Mr Carring, vainly wishing he'd come for her once more.

He had not.

Ellen grimaced at the disappointment.

The smell of cooking lamb stew drifted through the schoolhouse from the kitchen. Cooking meals had taken up a nice portion of the day. She was glad Mrs Sneddon had taught her cooking skills. After her father had lost their money, food had been problematic in their household, as her mother had never learned the skill, always relying on staff. Ellen was pleased she had learned the skill herself.

She sank down on an overstuffed library chair and picked up a book. She'd been reading to try and distract her thoughts from Mr Carring. Yet every male character in the books took his form, every poem she read seemed to be about him. *Them.*

She was infatuated with him, she realised, and it was entirely inconvenient. Every time she closed her eyes, she could see his fine, muscled chest, and feel his soft kisses on her neck.

She groaned and slammed the book down.

It was at that moment, she heard the front door chime. She stood and strode towards the window. She looked out, and there, standing on the street, was Mr Carring.

Her heart began to race, and between her legs liquified.

Lord. What was he doing?

Straightening her mob-cap, Ellen brushed down her dress and went to the front door.

***

It had taken Robert days to decide upon an appropriate ruse for him to visit the school. It had not been until Penelope had mentioned Miss Brampton was considering taking the girls on an excursion to Scotland in the summer that he formulated a plan.

He told Penelope he was going out for the day, and that in his travels he would stop by Miss Brampton's and drop of a letter of invitation. The Carrings had an estate in Inverness, and he would invite Miss Brampton to use it for the girls' excursion. The Sneddons could forward the letter to Miss Brampton's winter address.

He dressed in his fine coat and hat, and took the hack to Hackney Road.

When he arrived at the school, he was relieved to see the curtains on the second storey open, and knew Miss Smith must be in residence. Since their meeting, he had thought of nothing and no one but her. She was clever and passionate. Everything he could want in a woman, except she was devoted to her calling as a schoolteacher. Even that he admired. Still, if he could not have her formally, he would quite happily have her in whatever capacity he was able.

He tugged the bellpull, and heard the ring echo throughout the empty schoolhouse. The snow from the other day had turned to slush and ice, and it was freezing.

After a short time, the door opened.

Dressed in neat but unfashionable school dress, Ellen's face was stern, every bit the schoolmarm, and an enormous mob-cap covered her beautiful hair.

'Mr Carring?' she said. Only the breathlessness in her voice hinted at her true emotions.

'Miss Smith, may I come in? I have a letter of invitation for Miss Brampton.'

Beneath the hideous mob-cap, Ellen's brows collapsed.

'Of course,' she said softly, 'come in.'

Robert thought his heart may explode from his chest with the nerves.

He dusted his greatcoat and hung it on the coat stand, as Ellen closed and latched the door behind him.

As she turned he hung up his hat, and inclined his head, 'I'm sorry. I know you will be cross, but I simply had to see you...' Robert began; he gestured to the envelope in his hand.

He had not finished before Ellen threw herself into his arms. He caught her and the envelope fluttered to the floor, discarded. He drew her into him close, crushing her against his chest and kissing her passionately.

They kissed for an age, exploring, tasting, revelling in one another.

'Don't be sorry,' Ellen breathed, 'I am so glad you have come. I have been dreaming of this moment.'

Her small hands snaked under his jacket, hot and hungry.

He laughed into her kiss and allowed his own hands to move towards the despised cap. As they kissed, his hands moved under the lace and cotton contraption, deftly removing pins and finally freeing the scented riot of her curls. He let it fall to the floor.

Ellen pulled away.

'Robert ... we really shouldn't,' her cheeks were pink and her eyes were bright.

'The Sneddons, are they returned?' he asked.

She shook her head. 'No.'

'Then take me to your room, I'll stay just this one afternoon, then retreat from the servants' quarters. No one will be any the wiser. We shan't do it again.'

It was a lie and they both knew it.

He'd find other excuses to see her, and she'd find reasons to accept him.

She looked uncertain for just a moment and nodded. 'Very well.'

Then, with a soft laugh of excitement, she gripped his hand and pulled him up the stairwell, leaving the mob-cap and pins discarded on the lobby floor.

Ellen's room was warm, neat, and packed to capacity with books. The bed was thickly covered in quilts and pillows and her dressing table neatly stocked with all manner of feminine accoutrements.

'This is very comfortable,' he said as she closed the door behind them.

'It is,' she agreed.

He walked up behind her and wrapped his arms around her, her buttocks pressed into him. He groaned and pushed aside her hair and kissed her neck.

'I've missed you,' he whispered, kissing up her ear.

'As I have missed you,' she breathed.

His heart sang at her admission.

'You have enchanted me, Miss Ellen Smith,' he continued and chuckled as he felt her backside grind into his groin.

'Is that so, Mr Robert Carring,' she teased, suddenly utterly grateful of the empty schoolhouse, so no one could hear her scream his name.

'It is so,' he murmured and bent to pick up her skirts. As he lifted them, he gazed at the stocking-clad legs, and the round plump buttocks beneath. 'If you would be so kind as to hold these just a moment?' He moved her hands to hold up the skirts, as he unbuttoned his breeches.

She laughed throatily. 'Certainly,' she replied, and gripped the fabric high at her waist.

Robert's cock sprang free, moisture already beading at its head.

'Now, if you would just lean over the bed there, please. There is no time to waste.'

'Seeing as you asked so nicely, I will oblige,' she laughed again and did as he bid, leaning over the bed, raising her backside high in the air. Slick excitement wet the curls around her sex. Robert groaned, and stepped up behind her.

Deftly he parted the lips of her womanhood with one hand and guided the thick head of his cock with the other.

'You must hurry, no time to waste...' she moaned, as he pushed the ruddy head of his manhood past the open lips and dripping curls. He watched her flesh swallow him, gulping the broad length of cock almost to its hilt. 'Oh Robert, yes.'

He withdrew and pushed in again, her channel swallowed him like a silken glove. He thrust again, and withdrew and with each subsequent thrust, her cries grew louder.

'Yes,' she moaned, as his thighs smacked against her buttocks, 'Yes.'

***

Ellen pressed her head against the bed, revelling in the sensations Robert's new style of lovemaking offered. Soon the pressure and pleasure began to build, and she was fast losing sensibility.

Then she heard it, a door closed and heavy footsteps fell on wooden floorboards. The sound was faint, but distinct. She gasped.

Robert must have heard the same thing, he froze mid stroke.

'Miss Smith?' an elderly voice called.

Ellen's heart leapt into her mouth and she scrabbled madly away from Robert. Her skirts fell in a tumble.

Robert's eyes widened, and his hands flew to his cock, tucking it into his unbuttoned breeches.

'Miss Smith?' Mrs Sneddon knocked on the door. 'Are you in there?'

Aghast, Ellen stared at the unlatched door. 'Hide!' she whispered frantically.

Robert needed no urging. It would only be a moment or two before Mrs Sneddon tried the door and found it unlocked.

'Mrs Sneddon?' Ellen called breathlessly.

'Are ye all right? We found your cap on the floor in the lobby and an envelope. We were worried.'

Ellen turned to see Robert wrap himself behind the curtains, and laid down on the bed.

'I ... I ... am fine. I just had a funny turn. If you'd just give me a moment...'

Mrs Sneddon did not give her a moment, the doorknob twisted and she strode in.

The old woman gave Ellen a shrewd appraisal.

'Ye look flushed.' She grumbled. 'I knew I ought not leave you by yourself so long.' The old lady pressed a hand to Ellen's damp forehead.

'Ooh, that looks like the beginnings of a fever! To bed with you!'

Mrs Sneddon's gaze travelled to rumpled bed on which she lay, 'Go on, take off your uniform, and get abed.' She glanced towards the curtains, 'Your window is closed, isn't it? No point getting a chill on top of a fever.'

'Yes!' Ellen squeaked, 'Yes, the window is closed.' She unbuttoned her dress and stays and slipped into the bed. 'Really, Mrs Sneddon, I'm quite well.'

'Hmph,' Mrs Sneddon chuntered, and pulled back the bedspread and helped Ellen slip in.

'Truly, I'm fine, I've even made supper.'

'And it's burnt.' Mrs Sneddon frowned, 'Lucky we did come home, else you'd have burnt the whole school down.'

Ellen felt the colour roar up her cheeks. 'I...'

'You had a funny turn, I know. Get some rest, I'll be up with a cup of tea shortly.'

When Mrs Sneddon had deemed Ellen decently tucked in, she threw another shovel of coal on the fire and departed.

It was only as Mrs Sneddon's footstep receded down the corridor that Robert came out. His face was pale.

'You need to leave, and never come back!' Ellen hissed. 'This was a terrible idea!'

'Ellen,' Robert began, then closed his eyes as if just realising something. 'My greatcoat and hat are still in the lobby.'

Ellen's stomach plummeted. If the devout Catholic Mrs Sneddon discovered what she had been up to, she was ruined, but how could she explain the presence of a gentleman's coat and hat?

'You must leave, forget about them, I'll think of an excuse, but Robert, really, this is too close! We were almost caught.'

Robert's face creased with frustration. 'I know,' he agreed.

'The servants' exit is just down the corridor from the kitchen, it unlocks from the inside. Go whilst Mrs Sneddon busy in the kitchen.'

Robert nodded, and moved silently to the door. 'I'm sorry about this, Ellen,' he said, and quietly opened the door and slipped away.

Not ten minutes later, Mrs Sneddon bustled back into Ellen's room. She was feeling ill in earnest now. Her stomach was churning.

Deep lines creased the woman's brow. 'Along with your mob-cap, I see there's a gentleman's coat and hat in the lobby,' she said placing the tea, and Carring's unopened letter to Miss Brampton on the bedside table.

Ellen's heart thumped loudly. She held Mrs Sneddon's stern gaze.

'It belongs to Mr Carring, Penelope Carring's father,' she said, erring on the side of caution by telling as much truth as she could.

'Mr Carring, is it?' Mrs Sneddon scowled. 'A man like him doesn't seem like the forgetful sort. Why did he leave his things?' she pressed and her eyes narrowed to small slits. 'You'd not be the first schoolteacher to find yourself seduced by a dashing widower, but you'll be the last at Miss Brampton's if you have.' She warned.

Ellen glared at the woman. 'I most certainly have not been seduced.' She snapped, for in truth, she'd done the seducing. 'I merely offered him and Penelope tea when they came to deliver Miss Brampton's letter,' Ellen began haltingly. 'But Penelope fell faint and they had to depart quickly. I suppose in the ruckus he forgot his things.'

'Hmph,' Mrs Sneddon scowled. 'Well, you'd best get some rest. I'll bring up your porridge in the morning.'

Chapter 12

The next week was dark for Ellen. She wanted to reflect and daydream over the glorious, delicious moments with Mr Carring, rather than their awkward, embarrassed and hurried parting. The malaise she had feigned for Mrs Sneddon had developed into something very real, and she felt continuously ill and achy. Her monthly course was due any day, but nothing had happened—though her belly was cramping, giving every indication it would. Even Mrs Sneddon's chicken soup had done little to cheer her.

Ellen placed her book down on her lap, and stared into the fire, the uneasiness in her stomach growing.

As an educator of young women, Ellen knew at some level that what she had done so rashly with Mr Carring could result in a child. She had warned her girls of ruination through unwed pregnancy and now, though it was too early to tell, she may face the very outcome she'd warned her pupils so earnestly about.

No. Such a thing could not happen to her; after all, they had only been intimate three times. Was that enough? She'd known couples married for years without children. Would God be so cruel to inflict her after three glorious couplings, in one of which neither had reached completion?

She didn't know.

***

It had been over a week since Robert had visited Hackney Road. He'd very nearly been caught by Mr Sneddon as he'd slipped out the servants' entrance. It had only been through sheer luck that a flock of pigeons had fluttered overhead, distracting the old man and allowing Carring to get out of the garden gate unnoticed.

Every night, he had lain awake to the early hours thinking of Ellen, wondering about her, and hoping she was well.

How had she managed to explain the greatcoat and hat?

He sighed; she was clever, she would have thought of something.

Still, the need to see her was consuming him. Never in his life had he been so smitten by a woman. He could scarce tolerate the notion of living a life without her vitality and passion in it. Such an existence would be intolerably lonely and dull.

It was Monday evening, and Robert sighed and rested his head back in the chair, and listened to Penny play pianoforte. The scent of the pomanders Penny had made was rich and spicy in the air, and the foliage of the Christmas decorations green and shiny. The room was festive, cheerful, but missed a wife's touch.

I could marry Miss Smith.

Court her properly.

Robert sipped his brandy, swilling it around his glass and watching the rich amber fluid spin, and mulled over the notion.

'Penelope,' he asked, 'Do you wish me to remarry?'

Her playing stopped and her eyes brightened. 'Is there someone? Is that where you've been going lately?' she asked breathlessly. 'Oh Papa, I should love to have a stepmother!'

He laughed. 'Do not be so brash, Penelope. I confess there is a lady whom I admire. Alas, I have been given no indication of her interest in me.'

Penelope's face fell, 'Oh, I find that very hard to believe Papa, you are very handsome! Have you asked her how she feels?'

Robert stared at her—of all the sensual moments he had shared with Ellen, in not one had they spoken about marriage or matters of the heart. She'd given him no indication of such a desire. Nor even of her feelings towards him. She'd only ever spoken of her teaching, of being Miss Brampton's protégé.

Still, he could only ask and find out if she did feel the same way. At this point in their *dalliance* he had nothing at all to lose and everything to gain.

He was decided. He must return to Hackney Road.

***

Ellen retired without supper. Her courses should have arrived days ago. Her breasts were tender, and her stomach swilled with unrelenting nausea.

She knew the symptoms of being with child. Her neighbour had delivered sixteen children and had suffered through each confinement. She grimaced.

No, she didn't need any more confirmation. She was with child, she knew it as she knew her own silly, frivolous heart.

Slick fat tears rolled down her cheeks. She was ruined, utterly ruined.

Those glorious, dreamlike moments with Carring had turned her life into a growing nightmare.

Now she would undoubtedly lose her position at Miss Brampton's, as well as her position in society. She would become destitute.

Oh what have I done!

It would be humiliation beyond all humiliations. Ellen sniffed and ran a hand through her tangled hair and buried her face in her bed.

And yet, despite it all, she still wanted Mr Carring to be hers with an ache so deep she could feel it in her very bones. She missed him, she missed their banter. She missed the way his eyes brightened when he saw her.

'Are ye or'right?' Mr Sneddon knocked at her door. 'Ye not eaten yer tea.'

'I'm just under the weather, Mr Sneddon, I shall be fine tomorrow,' she choked out. Hot tears fell down her cheeks at the lie. Tomorrow, Christmas Eve, she would be but one day closer to ruination.

She could hear Mr Sneddon huff, 'Ye coming to mass with us in the morning?' he said.

Mass? So God and his blasted angels could scorn her?

She'd thrown away a perfectly safe, good existence for silly, foolish pleasures. She deserved all the curses God could throw.

And Mr Carring! What would he think? Would he ever want her again knowing what a fool she'd been?

She choked back another sob.

'Well?' Mr Sneddon asked again through the door.

'Of course, I should like that very much. You're ... you're too kind.' she sniffed.

How much of their kindness would remain when they watched her belly swell without a husband to protect it? 'Goodnight, Mr Sneddon,' she croaked.

'Or'right love, I'll lock up and head off then, goodnight,' he added and Ellen listened to him shuffle down the stairs and head towards his cottage at the back.

She lay there for hours, or for what seemed like hours.

What the devil should she do? Should she remain in Miss Brampton's employ until her condition became too obvious, then throw herself on Miss Brampton's mercy?

She imagined the confrontation. Swollen with a mystery bastard, Miss Brampton would be appalled. She'd be thrown out unceremoniously, for the school founder would have no sympathy, none, she knew. Miss Brampton was a good Catholic woman, children were a blessing, but a woman breeding out of wedlock was an unforgiveable sin. Another hot tear leaked from her eye and pooled in her ear, as she lay abed thinking of the shame. What in heaven's name was she thinking allowing herself to fornicate with Mr Carring?

Yet given the chance, she'd probably do the same thing again. To be the object of Mr Carring's passion and attention had made her feel more alive in minutes than she had in her entire life.

You mustn't think like that. She warned herself. Such thoughts were pointless, even irrelevant now.

Perhaps she should just flee, take what meagre savings she possessed and start a life somewhere else, citing she was a young widow.

Ellen dried her eyes on her blanket and considered. In the savings tin beneath her bed, she had enough funds to rent a room somewhere, she knew, but those funds would stretch thin quickly, especially with a baby and no means of honestly supporting herself. No school would hire a teacher with a babe on teat. Even she knew the notion was ridiculous.

Ellen rolled over and screamed into the soft down of her pillow. Frustration warred with nausea in her belly and a cloying sense of desperation covered her heavier than a lead blanket.

The situation was untenable. She had but one option: tomorrow, Christmas Eve, she would throw herself on Mr Carring's mercy. He was a good man, and kind father.

She would beg him to take care of the child.

Chapter 13

Robert Carring did not wait another moment.

He could not.

He had to discover what Miss Smith felt for him. If it was anything like the affection he held for her, then surely she would give marriage a chance.

Much to Penelope's surprise, he donned a coat and hat.

'Papa, what are you doing? It is snowing outside. Surely you aren't going for a walk?' she asked, her hands resting on the keys of the pianoforte.

'I shall take the hack. There is something I must do,' he declared as he kissed his daughter on the cheek.

'Can it not wait? It is Christmas Eve tomorrow.'

A sense of urgency rose in his chest. 'No, it cannot wait, wish me well.'

Penelope's pretty face contorted in surprise. 'I would wish you well, if I knew where you were going or what you were doing, but I do not!' she exclaimed. 'You are very strange, Papa,' she added.

Robert laughed and called for his hack.

Ten minutes later, he raced the hack through the streets, determined to reach Miss Brampton's school before it was too late in the evening to be at all civil.

His hack drew up outside Miss Brampton's, and he knew it was already an uncivil time to call unannounced.

The building was entirely dark, except beyond the closed curtains on the second floor, a lamplight shone. Ellen's bedroom.

He hesitated. Perhaps she would not be pleased to see him at this hour?

Perhaps he should call in the morning after all?

A shadow moved behind the curtain, his heart contracted, and his doubts dissolved.

He bit his lip and leapt down from the hack.

Devil take him, he may look a fool, but he could not sleep another night not knowing how she felt. His hands trembled slightly as he tied the horse's reins to a post, and glanced up again at the window.

Nothing moved now.

Robert strode purposefully to the door of the school. As his hand hesitated on the bellpull, he thought of what he might say. If it were not Miss Smith and the elderly Sneddons answered, what would his excuse be?

He was here to pick up his coat and hat?

Ugh. No, that could be dangerous.

His hand hesitated again, what the devil would he say?

His horse was lame, and he was too tired to walk home, perhaps Mr Sneddon could look over his animal?

That could work.

Decided, Robert pulled the bell. Beyond the rattle of traffic and hum of late evening activity in the street, he could hear the bell echo throughout the empty schoolhouse.

He pulled the bellpull a second time.

The chime rang on, empty and hollow. It reminded him of all the things he'd been missing without her and of all the things he wanted to share, with someone, with her.

A carriage rolled past and a small group of Christmas revellers wandered along the cobbles towards him. He tipped his hat at them and dared a glance up at the window once more.

He could hear no footsteps in the schoolhouse, but the curtain on the second floor moved, and a face peered down.

The face was small and shrouded in a riot of blonde curls that haloed her shadowed face.

'Miss Smith?'

At his call, the figure jerked in surprise and her hands moved quickly to open the window. He heard the sound of the window sash squeak as it rose. His heart beat even faster. 'Forgive me, I had to call.'

***

Ellen was frozen with surprise: Mr Carring stood in the street below, tall and determined. Her heart thumped with wild affection.

But what was he doing? Why was he here?

She had hoped to visit him on the morrow and plea her humiliating case, but now, in the cold winter night, the notion seemed ridiculous and destined for failure. How could she ever have expected a man as strong and proud as Mr Carring to ever listen to the pleas of a tarnished woman?

I ought to send him on his way.

'Mr Carring, what are you doing?' she asked, 'Why are you here?'

She was only grateful the Sneddons had retired early for the night to their cottage.

'I simply must speak with you, bedamned what anyone thinks.'

Her throat tightened, what was he saying?

'Come in, but you must be quiet,' she said, looking up and down the street, praying no one was eavesdropping.

Hurriedly, Ellen closed the window and gathered her warmest shawl and tiptoed down the stairs and unlatched the front door.

Carring swept in, wrapping his arms around her and kissing her.

For the first time, she could not reciprocate his passion; nausea swilled in her belly and hot humiliation burnt up her throat. She had been such a fool to ever think she could treat herself to pleasure without paying the price.

She was ruined, soon enough he would find her repulsive.

She pulled away from him. 'Robert, I am carrying your child,' she said.

***

Robert felt her stiffen and pull away. He looked down at her, perplexed. Even by the light of her single oil lamp, she looked deathly pale.

'I am carrying your child,' she repeated.

His heart slowed to a loud thud in his head.

Of the many, varied things he'd expected Miss Smith to say, confessing pregnancy was not one of them. In truth, he wasn't sure what he'd expected upon his arrival. Anger that he'd come to visit her against her wishes, or excitement that he had. What he hadn't expected was to be informed of impending fatherhood.

He stared at her, vaguely aware his mouth was slightly agape.

His beautiful Ellen, brave, frank and honest.

Words were lost to him. He attempted to express his amazement, but his tongue tripped in his mouth.

'Don't say anything. Let me speak before I lose my composure all together,' she moved closer once again, her expression pleading.

At this proximity he could smell her lavender scent, and his body stirred at the memories. How he wanted her. How he adored her. He had waited for this moment for weeks.

'You must know, I hold you in my deepest affections.' she began.

Carring felt a smile turn the corner of his lips.

She did care for him!

'And I beg you not to think ill of me.'

He frowned, he did not think ill of her. *He could not!*

Despite her unconventional behaviour and condition, she had brought joy and excitement back to his world, with just one night. She had reminded him that he was alive, that he could *feel*.

If that is the joy she can bring in one night, what magic could we share in a lifetime?

Ellen continued, 'As I have told you, that night of passion was a Christmas gift to myself. I am ... *was* ... to become Miss Brampton's replacement, yet I could not tolerate the notion of living a life half lived, so before I committed myself entirely to spinsterhood—I gifted myself one evening with which to dance and make merry. I never intended on seducing you. Or ever letting it happen again. I was maiden, I had no understanding of pleasure, yet being with you has brought me more joy in one month than I had hoped to find in a lifetime...' She faded, and finished in a whisper, 'I don't expect anything from you, what I have done I did on my own, but this child is innocent and I beg you from the deepest part of my soul to please take care of it...' Tears began to spill down her pale cheeks, 'I should regret it, I should beg your forgiveness for the child's sake, if not my own, but in truth,' she sobbed, 'I'd do it all again just to be with you one more time.'

Her hands covered her face and she sobbed softly.

A fierce sense of protectiveness swooped over Robert's body and settled in his chest.

'You regret nothing? Even though you are with my child?' he asked.

She looked up at him, her eyes glittering with tears.

'I regret nothing,' she whispered, 'though I most certainly should.'

Robert smiled at her, 'I love you, my brave, clever, utterly unconventional, Miss Ellen Smith, marry me, be my Christmas bride,' he said and kissed her.

***

There were many things in her life that Ellen Smith had doubts about; the solemnity and dullness of her career as a spinster schoolmarm, the situation that had led to her giving her maidenhead to Mr Carring in a dirty alley that chilly London night. She even had doubts that dear Mr Carring could procure a wedding license at Christmas, and at such short notice.

But she had no doubts now.

Dressed in a sweet, fawn-coloured bridal gown, hastily altered by Mrs Mathers, Robert's housekeeper, Ellen stood before the altar at St James's Church with Mr Robert Carring by her side.

She felt like the luckiest woman alive. She had found a man who loved her and who she loved ardently in return. Of course, she'd have to disappoint Miss Brampton, but there were others much more deserving and needing of that position.

She felt Robert's gaze on her, warm, affectionate and hungry all at once. Excited gooseflesh rippled down her arms.

Nothing had felt more right to her. Penelope beamed delightedly from the pews, whilst a shocked Mr and Mrs Sneddon sat alongside.

It was hard to believe that her Christmas gift to herself had resulted in a gift for not only Mr Carring but his family as well. Their baby. She touched her belly lightly. Robert caught the gesture and a proud smile played on the corners of his lips.

The priest's voice was calm and clear in the nearly empty church.

'I require and charge you both, as ye will answer at the dreadful day of judgement when the secrets of all hearts shall be disclosed, that if either of you know any impediment why ye may not be lawfully joined together in matrimony, ye do now confess it. For be ye well assured, that if any persons are joined together otherwise than as God's Word doth allow, their marriage is not lawful.'

The church was silent. Some silly part of her half expected someone to voice word of her pregnancy, and renounce her as a charlatan, but all was gratefully silent.

Her shoulders softened and she caught Robert's eyes again. His lips curled in a deeper, more secretive smile, and she could not help but smile in return.

The priest turned to Robert, 'Wilt thou, Robert Rushforth Carring, have this woman to thy wedded wife, to live together after God's ordinance in the holy estate of matrimony? Wilt thou love her, comfort her honour and keep her in sickness and in health, and, forsaking all others, keep thee only unto her, so long as ye both shall live?'

Robert took her hand. It was warm and firm. She looked up into his dark-fringed hazel eyes to find they were brimming with emotion. 'I will,' he said.

Tears pricked in her own eyes; this man had devoted himself to *her* alone. It was almost incomprehensible, after their short, passionate encounter.

The priest turned his gaze towards her, and began again, 'Wilt thou, Ellen Mary Smith, have this man to thy wedded husband, to live together after God's ordinance in the holy estate of matrimony? Wilt thou obey him, and serve him, love, honour, and keep him in sickness and in health; and, forsaking all others, keep thee only unto him, so long as ye both shall live?'

She thought of the past month, the tormenting dreams, long nights and lonely days, and knew neither he nor she would ever suffer such agonies again.

'I will,' she said.

Then he kissed her.

When Robert pulled away, a delighted laugh burbled up her throat. A Christmas wedding was an entirely irregular start to a marriage but Robert smiled at her, revelling in her joy. Despite the disapproving glare of the priest, Ellen laughed a little louder. She cared not what the priest, nor anyone else, thought of their unconventional marriage. After all, she was an entirely unconventional lady.

Thanks for reading **A Christmas Bride.** I hope you enjoyed it..

Reviews can help readers find books, and I am grateful for all honest reviews. Thank you for taking the time to let others know what you've read, and what you thought.

If you liked this book, here are my other books, ***The Secret Diary of Lady Catherine Bexley, The Wicked Confessions of Lady Cecelia Stanton, The Private Affairs of Lady Jane Fielding, The Observations of a Curious Governess, The Journal of a Vicar's Wife.***

Sign up to our newsletter romance. com.au/newsletter/ and find out about new releases, must-read series and ***ebook deals*** at romance.com.au.

Share your reading experience on:

Facebook
Instagram
romance.com.au

ROMANCE .COM.AU ESCAPE publishing A novel approach

Bestselling Titles by Escape Publishing...

Discover another great read from Escape publishing....

Wicked Confessions

Viveka Portman

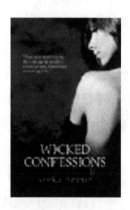

Regency England: appearance is everything ... but underneath lies a seething world of unexpected desire, unshared fantasies and uncontrollable lust.

Three deliciously erotic stories to indulge the senses and incite the imagination:

When faced with a rakish, lusty husband, what is a proper English wife to do but educate herself in the art of bedplay? **Lady Cecelia Stanton** is married to the dashing and philandering Lord Stanton, a situation that would distress even the most composed and refined gently born lady. However, Cecelia has a secret balm for her dissatisfaction...

Lady Catherine Bexley is new to marriage and the marriage bed, but surely there must be more to it than this? Her husband is proper and perfunctory – treating her with careful respect but leaving her aching for more. Soon, though, she develops a naughty plan to finally get what she wants...

In the world of Regency England, only one thing matters – the begetting of an heir. But Lord Jacob Fielding and his wife **Jane Fielding** have only daughters. In desperation, Lord Fielding formulates a wicked plan. He invites his distant cousin Matthew to come and share their home ... and possibly more.

Journal of a Vicar's Wife

Viveka Portman

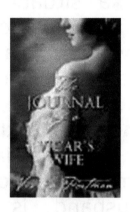

The latest instalment in Viveka Portman's sexy, sinful *Regency Diaries* sees an unhappy wife desperately seeking love–and her taciturn husband who doesn't know how to reach her.

My husband, though I do not doubt his goodness, does not love nor want me. He married me for pure convenience. He needed a bride and I was the one offered to him. Thus I find my pleasures where I may...

Mrs Maria Reeves has been married for six years. Six long, lonely years. She craves love and affection, but married to a handsome but pious vicar she receives little in the way of earthly pleasures. The Reverend Vicar Frederick Reeves is a man of principle and morals, and is more likely to provide his wife with suggested Bible readings than carnal knowledge.

If her husband will not please her, then she will find a man who will.

But infidelity doesn't come naturally to the vicar's wife. Though Maria finds herself getting the sexual pleasure she desires, she also finds herself emotionally frayed and unhappy. To make matters worse, in the small village of Stanton there are always people watching, and Maria discovers that some secrets are impossible to keep. What will her upright husband do when he discovers that Maria has broken not only one of the commandments, but her vows to him?

The Observations of a Curious Governess

Viveka Portman

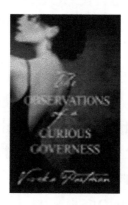

Viveka Portman's latest instalment in the sexiest set of diaries you have ever read...

When Miss Martha Swan enters the fine home of Lord and Lady Stanton to become a governess, she is full of lofty ideals. Yet something is amiss in the hallowed halls of Stanton: whispers, laughter, and something darker and more wicked echoes from behind closed doors, and Martha is determined to find out what.

She soon discovers that all is not as it seems in this stately home. The lord and lady have secrets—lustful, carnal, shameful secrets that could spell ruination for all. Martha wants to be appalled, but she finds herself intrigued, and when her long-time friend Mr Jonathan Reeves comes to visit, Martha conceives a daring plan to assuage her curiosity.

Thing are not so simple however, as neither Martha nor Jonathan have the money to marry. Nothing can come from this relationship—nothing but the experience of ecstasy. In such a situation, what is a curious governess to do?

CPSIA information can be obtained
at www.ICGtesting.com
Printed in the USA
BVHW050804140223
658473BV00005B/135